'That will be all, Nurse, and I'm afraid it's not open to discussion. I shall expect your resignation on my desk today, and you must leave at the end of the week.'

Vivien got up feeling dazed. It was a shattering blow, and as she came out of the office her eyes were stinging with unshed tears. Sacked from the job she'd entered with so much interest and such high hopes. Just because she'd obliged a friend!

She was suddenly swept by a burning anger towards Dr Justin Baron, since it gave her someone to blame besides herself. It *was* his fault. If he hadn't turned up here and given Vivien away, she would still have a job!

She swept back into the ward feeling angry and sore-hearted and with rage consuming her so much that she felt like walking straight up to him and giving him a piece of her mind. Why had she felt so pleased to see him? He had no business to be here, and it just wasn't fair!

Barbara Perkins began writing when her children were small as a way of combining her nursing training with an earlier ambition to be a writer. The children are grown up now but Barbara still writes Doctor-Nurse Romances because, she says, hospitals are fascinating worlds of their own, and where else would you find all the ingredients of drama under one roof? Modern nursing information comes from friends still in the profession and from a daughter-in-law who is a nurse. Barbara lives near the sea in Kent.

ISLAND OF HEALING

BY

BARBARA PERKINS

MILLS & BOON LIMITED
ETON HOUSE 18–24 PARADISE ROAD
RICHMOND SURREY TW9 1SR

All the characters in this book have no existence outside the imagination of the Author, and have no relation whatsoever to anyone bearing the same name or names. They are not even distantly inspired by any individual known or unknown to the Author, and all the incidents are pure invention.

First published in Great Britain 1987
by Mills & Boon Limited

ISBN 0 263 76014 6

Set in 10 on 11 pt Linotron Times
03–0288–57,800

Photoset by Rowland Phototypesetting Limited
Bury St Edmunds, Suffolk
Made and printed in Great Britain by
William Collins Sons & Co Limited, Glasgow

CHAPTER ONE

'AREN'T you sorry it's your last week of agency nursing, Vivi?' asked Caroline, as the two of them dashed round their shared flat getting ready for a night duty. 'Personally, I wouldn't go back to a hospital job for anything!'

Vivien's dark blue eyes narrowed with a rueful gleam. 'You mean because it's less money? I know, but all the same I like hospital work. I've missed it since we qualified six months ago. Not that I'm not grateful to the agency for giving me the extra experience, but . . .'

'All the same you'd rather be getting back to our old stamping ground?'

'You know me, a down-to-earth type! Besides, it's a good job and promises to be interesting—staff nurse in the leukaemia unit.' Vivien glanced across with a grin. 'A step on the career ladder instead of flitting around like a butterfly amongst the halls of fame!'

'Is that a crack, by any chance? Because you saw me flirting with one of the doctors last week? One thing about private work, you do run into some of the richer and dishier medical types, don't you?' Caroline giggled and tossed the blonde curls which contrasted so effectively with her soft brown eyes. 'Come on, are you ready to go? Have I got everything? Let's see, agency label, cap, uniform cardigan——Brr, I wish winter would hurry up and finish, don't you?'

They looked a tidy but contrasting pair as they both ran down the stairs from their top-floor flat which looked out on to anonymous London streets and a tiny glimpse of a local park. Both wore navy raincoats belted over white agency nursing overalls with black tights to show off neat ankles, and sensible shoes; both were much of a height; but Caroline was all curvy figure and blonde curls, while Vivien was aware of herself as being much more ordinary with her long dark hair pinned neatly up into a tidy coil, her straight dark eyebrows above blue eyes, the mouth which always seemed to her to be too wide above a short chin and long neck. She didn't resent Caroline's chocolate-box prettiness, but she was wryly aware of her own shortcomings by comparison. They had been friends ever since they started training together and had shared all their major and minor triumphs and heartbreaks.

Caroline was chattering away as they leapt on to the bus which would take them to their destination. 'I shouldn't sign off from the agency's books if I were you. You may want to do some moonlighting. Quite a lot of people are going in for that, aren't they? If you're on a ten-days-on followed by seven off it gives you time. Hey, did I tell you . . .'

She flitted off on to another subject, but as she listened with half an ear Vivien thought she probably wouldn't go in for moonlighting. The nursing officers seemed to turn a blind eye to it from what she had heard, but it still seemed slightly dubious to combine two jobs when one was likely to be intensive enough. Then she forgot the whole question as they arrived in the quiet street which held the North London Nursing Home, and went to sign in for the night's work.

Vivien's patient for the night was an Arab lady, semi-comatose after an abdominal resection. Her notes didn't look very promising, with secondaries mentioned, and she had both a surgeon and a physician named on her notes. When she woke there was a certain trouble with language since the patient had very little English, but she seemed reassured by her nurse's quiet manner and they managed to get by with signs.

It was a quiet night, the usual twelve-hour shift from

eight p.m. to eight a.m. There was little for Vivien to do except administer a morphine injection at stated intervals if her patient woke up in pain. At seven in the morning Mrs Kahreini woke more thoroughly, and since an injection wasn't due Vivien sponged her face and hands gently to freshen her up. She had just completed that when the door of the private room opened quietly. She glanced round with the beginning of a smile for the nursing officer who must be making her morning rounds. Then she found her breath caught involuntarily, half disconcerted and half in surprise at the sight of the man who had entered.

He was extraordinarily striking by anyone's standards, and particularly at this time in the morning; elegantly dressed in a pale grey suit with a dazzlingly white shirt and a discreetly-expensive-looking tie. He looked meticulously shaven, and the faintest tang of a clear fresh aftershave reached Vivien as he came forward with a brief nod in her direction. Pale skin contrasted with smoothly tidy black hair with just a hint of a curl in it, but it was his eyes which gave a handsome face a particular distinction. They were oddly light, an unusual and distinct green.

He lifted the notes from their position on a hook at the end of the bed without speaking and took a quick glance through them. Mrs Kahreini's dulled eyes had brightened a little at the sight of him and she began a broken sentence in her own language. As the newcomer answered her in the same soft gutturals Vivien reached the easy conclusion that this was one of her patient's doctors, and that if he too was an Arab that explained his slightly foreign look.

She couldn't help noticing too, with unconscious fascination, that he had an unusually pleasant speaking voice, light and somehow caressing in the foreign language. She almost jumped as he turned in her direction and switched to an accentless English.

'Has Mrs Kahreini shown much discomfort before the analgesics were due? Enough to disturb her?'

'Not really, Dr——'

'Baron,' he supplied into her interrogatory pause.

'She seems to have slept quite well, Dr Baron, apart from the times I've logged at two and six when she was falling due for an injection anyway.'

'Good. She's due to fly home this evening on an ambulance flight—rather soon, but it looks as if we'll be able to fulfil the prior arrangement.'

Mrs Kahreini reached to tug at his sleeve and he turned back to her. There was a short conversation, then he patted the patient's hand and gave her a smile that lit his face with such dynamism that Vivien wouldn't have been at all surprised if Mrs Kahreini had bridled. Instead she settled back on her pillows and closed her eyes, leaving the doctor to turn away.

He was giving Vivien a thoughtful glance, and summoned her to go with him to the door with a casual wave of his hand. She did so obediently, only to find herself being even more thoroughly studied as he paused with his hand on the doorknob, and in a way that made her feel abruptly self-conscious.

'Mrs Kahreini wished me to pass on to you that you have very gentle hands, and a neck like a swan,' he said, deadpan—but there was a sudden glint of amusement somewhere in the depths of those unusual green eyes, and the way they were fixed on her sent Vivien's knees suddenly and ridiculously weak. She tried to pull herself together hastily, but he was going on. 'Not *quite* as long as a swan's, fortunately for you, but I see what she means . . .'

His amused, considering glance brought a vision unwarily into Vivien's mind: Dr Baron in a sheikh's headdress offering to sweep her off to a silken tent in the desert. She swallowed hard, her mouth twitching in involuntary amusement, and managed.

'Thank you, Dr Baron.'

'Arab compliments do tend to be flowery. On the other hand——'

Whatever he might have been about to say was interrupted as the door pushed against his hand. Caroline came round the door, then stopped abruptly.

'Oh, I'm sorry—wrong room——'

She gave Dr Baron one of her most enchanting smiles. With a feeling of inevitability, Vivien knew the doctor would fall prey to it.

Sure enough, as Caroline disappeared Dr Baron turned back to Vivien with a look which had smoothed out into impersonal formality.

'I think that's all, nurse. Good morning!'

The door closed behind him. Vivien bit her lip. Most of the doctors she worked for were undeniably middle-aged, and this much younger one had been worth anyone's appreciation: some five feet ten inches of compact muscularity with a strong jaw, that amazingly attractive smile, and those green eyes. She found she could visualise him so accurately that it was like an imprint left on a negative. Just her luck to run into something like that so briefly! She could even imagine rippling muscles under that dazzlingly white shirt——

She caught at her thoughts with a suppressed choke of amusement, deciding she really must be starved of male company to fall into an immediate dream about the first good-looking specimen she came across. Out of her league, too. It was probably her imagination that there had been a gleam of appreciation in his eyes—until Caroline turned up—and her blood sugar was probably low at this time in the morning, to send her thoughts in such unlikely directions. However, one *could* dream, she supposed!

Caroline's brief glimpse of Dr Baron seemed to have had just as striking an effect, and she began to bubble with questions as soon as she and Vivien met up to travel home together.

'Who was *that* I bumped into when I was coming in to see how you were getting on? What a dish! I wonder if he'll be in again tonight? I really must try to fall over him in the corridor if he is!'

'Tough luck, his patient's being discharged this evening. Still, I suppose he might turn up with another one. I suppose he did rather improve the landscape!'

'Oh, more than that—particularly compared with *my* patient's doctor, who was twice as old as Methuselah and all hands! Not the sort I want to be noticed by at all, whereas yours—mmm! I do like a man with a slightly dangerous look about him,' said Caroline with an unrepentant relish that made Vivien give a sleepy giggle.

'Honestly, Caroline, no one would think you were really so devoted to Tom!' she told her friend teasingly, but with a very light reproof. 'Tom, yes? *Your* Tom?'

Caroline and Dr Thomas Ainslie had been an inseparable pair for a year. It was almost difficult now to remember that Vivien had known him first. He had been a houseman on her ward and she had even hoped he was noticing her, in those far-off days. Then he had met Caroline at a party and her dazzling looks and bubbling personality had knocked him sideways. So that was that.

For the last three months, however, he had been acting as a locum GP in Edinburgh and keeping in touch with his lady-love by letters and long telephone calls. He was coming down soon, Vivien remembered, for a visit. That would take Caroline's mind off handsome private doctors!

A few days later Vivien had plenty else to think of herself as she plunged back into hospital life. The leukaemia unit with its small linked wards absorbed all her attention. New treatments seemed to be discovered almost daily, and Vivien found herself bringing notes home in the evening to study the latest advances in therapy. She wanted to do well in this job. The extra work, anyway, provided an excuse to withdraw to her room rather than feeling as if she was playing gooseberry; because Tom Ainslie arrived and seemed to take up a lot of room in the flat.

He had hitched down from Edinburgh overnight and arrived looking scruffy but cheerful, to seize Caroline into his arms immediately with a sigh of satisfaction. Six foot two and as fair as Caroline but with straight hair that flopped over his brow, he habitually looked something between a Viking and a poet. His slight air of helplessness had always made Vivien feel faintly maternal.

Over the next few days, and fond of him though she was, Vivien found herself feeling exasperated as much as maternal because he was underfoot so much—unshaven across the breakfast table, wandering through to the bathroom in his underpants, taking up much too much space in the minuscule kitchen. When he had been a hospital resident he had had his own accommodation, but now she was always tripping over him. Or over both him and Caroline, in a permanent state of affection about the place.

Vivien treated him in her usual sisterly fashion, and tried not to feel like a maiden aunt in the presence of two lovebirds. When, at last, it was time for him to go, he gave Vivien his usual brotherly peck on the cheek.

'Keep an eye on Caroline for me, won't you, Viv?' He cast a doting look at his beloved on the words. The slight Scots burr which had always been there in his voice seemed to have increased since his return to his native Edinburgh. 'And both of you take care of yourselves, mind!'

'Sure will!' Vivien told him brightly.

'Well, I must be off. It's a long hitch northwards, so let's hope the lorry-drivers are sympathetic. Caroline, angel, you're coming out to see me off, aren't you?'

He was as perennially broke as most young doctors, since he was saving up to buy himself into a practice.

When the two of them had gone with their arms wound round each other, Vivien looked round the sudden emptiness of the flat and was surprised to find herself feeling wistful rather than relieved.

Catching sight of herself in the mirror, she reflected wryly that she didn't *look* all that maiden-auntish, with the long dark hair which suited her better hanging loose, as now, than in its neat nursing coil. Her eyes were a reasonable size and shape, her features tolerably regular . . . She decided all at once that she really must start going to parties again and mixing. That would cure her of feeling dull, and stupid, and irritatingly wistful because Caroline was in love and she wasn't.

For a moment she had a vision of the handsome green-eyed Dr Baron, flitting into her mind as an involuntary memory. It was annoying that he should remain in her head as a comparison with the doctors on her ward—and equally annoying that it gave her a stab of regret to realise that. After all, she was unlikely ever to see him again. So it was silly to have to remind herself firmly that she did infinitely prefer working in the leukaemia unit to the constant change and variation of agency nursing.

She was settling down well. The leukaemia unit was modern and cheerful, and Vivien was currently spending at least half her working hours in the children's area. She didn't normally specialise in children, but she liked them.

'Ironic that you should be with kids when I'm the one who took a special training in them,' Caroline commented in one of the times when they ran across each other, rare now that they were working such different hours. 'I seem to have had nothing but geriatrics lately. Any interesting male talent on your ward?'

'None that I've particularly noticed. Two male nurses, both married; a registrar, ditto; a couple of plain housemen——'

'Spare me! The very young and still spotty kind? Oh, by the way, I know what I forgot to tell you! Remember that dishy doctor you worked for just before you finished agency? I ran into him again the other day, and I'd swear he remembered me! He seems to specialise in Arab patients. I'd almost have thought he was one himself, but he isn't: he's so dark because he's half Maltese.'

'Oh? Where did you glean that from—or did you ask him? What *was* his name?' Vivien asked airily, then wondered why she was lying when she could remember it perfectly well.

'Dr Baron. No, of course I didn't ask him, silly, I was just finding out a few things from the other nurses! His first name's Justin. With luck I'll run into him again, because I heard him asking some questions about agency nurses and whether particular ones were available, so I'm hoping he might have meant me! Well, I did take care to give him one of my best smiles when I ran into him in the corridor, so one can always hope!'

Vivien opened her mouth to mention pointedly the letter Caroline had had from Tom only that morning, but Caroline's words had brought something else to mind. 'That reminds me, I haven't written my official signing-off letter to the agency. No, Caroline, I really don't feel like moonlighting, even if it is extra money. I've got enough to keep me busy as it is!'

Vivien meant what she said, but a sudden rush of work sent the matter out of her head. If she could have dealt with it by a phone call that would have been one thing, but the nursing agency, being a highly respected one, expected a properly formal resignation letter. She certainly didn't mean to do any moonlighting whoever it meant she might meet. She wouldn't have, either, but for a crisis.

The weather had been awful; London in one of its bleak midwinter periods. Sleety rain slanted down in icy needles. An unremitting grey sky loured over grey wet buildings. Even the pigeons across the way from the top-floor Islington flat looked shrammed with cold. Vivien had just started a seven days off when Caroline arrived back from a night duty pale and shivering and bemoaning the fact that she'd got another duty booked for tonight. Then she woke up heavy-eyed and obviously running a temperature.

'You can't go on duty, Caroline, there's no question of that. I'll ring up for you and cancel it——'

'Oh, Vivi, you wouldn't go in for me, would you? You know what they're like about last-minute cancellations!'

'Don't be silly, they can't blame you for being genuinely ill!'

'Yes, but I've skipped out of one before without having a fill-in, and they didn't half fuss! That was for a date—I didn't tell you——'

'Serve you right,' said Vivien unsympathetically, but she looked at her frined with concern. 'Anyway, you can't possibly go tonight, and this one's genuine.'

'So was the other,' Caroline said with almost a touch of her usual bounce. 'It was that dishy Dr Baron—I said I'd get him, didn't I? Well, there I was, in the Post Office—the one nearest to Harley Street, you know? —when he came in. So I did my "Oh, hallo, it's you" act, and since it was just before lunchtime it kind of evolved into an invitation to the nearest pub—you know how these things go!'

'I know how they go when you're around!'

'I've been hoping ever since that he'd ring me. He's *very* smooth, and ultra-charming! And with that around I wasn't going to admit I was due on a three o'clock shift, now was I? So I made an excuse to slip off and ring the agency and said I wasn't well. They made a fuss *then* about the fact that I ought to have found my own replacement, and if I do it again, they might stop using me! So *please*, Vivi . . .'

It was on the tip of Vivien's tongue to say again

that it served her right, and to mention Tom lingering devotedly in the background. Vivien sighed, looked at her friend's feverish face, and gave in.

'Oh, all right, this once! You're lucky I'm on days off, so I suppose one night won't hurt me. I'll ring the agency and say I'm taking over from you, OK? But this really is the only time, and I wouldn't do it for anyone but you!'

'You're an angel,' Caroline said fervently. Her hand reached urgently to tug Vivien's sleeve. 'Oh, and listen, if he's there——'

'If *who's* there?'

'Justin, of course! Dr Baron to you. It's not his patient I'm supposed to be nursing, worse luck, but it *is* the North London Nursing Home again and he seems to use it quite a lot. That's what's so maddening about being ill tonight, I was hoping to run into him again.'

'And if he's there what am I supposed to do? Give him your love?'

'You needn't go that far,' said Caroline on a husky chuckle. 'No, I was only going to say if he's there, hands off, because I saw him first! He's obviously stinking rich as well as being charming—well, they all are when they specialise in private patients, aren't they, and his always seem to be Arabs! I can't help feeling it'd be a nice change to go out with someone who doesn't always have to choose the cheapest thing on the menu!'

Vivien winced to hear Caroline sound so mercenary, with the obvious comparison with Tom, who was always as broke as most young doctors. However, Caroline was already giving her a rueful look.

'All right, I know, I sound awful! But it isn't the money really, it's the man himself—I can't help finding him intriguing. He's worked all over the place, Middle East, America—and I told you, didn't I, that his mother's Maltese? From some rather posh family, I gather. His sister lives over there too. One of them—he said he'd got two. Both married, but *he* isn't.'

'You do seem to have grilled him thoroughly!'

'Make a point of getting a man to talk about himself, I always say. Mind you, we avoided shop, thank goodness. He really is a terrific charmer, and those eyes!'

'If I'm going to ring the agency I'd better go and do it,' Vivien said abruptly, and swept away quickly before her feelings could show in her face. The dreamy look in Caroline's eye really did seem unfair on Tom. Vivien told herself it was only that.

The agency didn't seem to mind changing the booking from Nurse C. Jones to Nurse V. Challock when both names were still on their books. Vivien went to reclaim one of the agency overalls she had passed on to Caroline, showered quickly, and pinned her hair back up into its duty coil with a small sigh. It was supposed to be her time off—but Caroline couldn't help going down with a temperature.

She *could* have helped skipping a previous duty for the sake of spending time with the glamorous Dr Justin Baron. Vivien rather hoped he wouldn't show up at the nursing home tonight. It would only remind her of what she already knew: that Caroline was far more noticeable than she was to the opposite sex.

She spent the night involuntarily looking out for him, and was irritated when she caught herself doing it. Her patient, a middle-aged man who had had his gall-bladder removed, was fussy and restless after the standard operation. When he had finally settled Vivien found her mind straying in the quiet to Dr Baron again, wondering what his speciality was. Something in the line of carcinomas or lymphadenomas, to judge from Mrs Kahreini. He wasn't a surgeon: he had been down as that patient's general doctor with someone else called in for the surgery.

Vivien shook her head crossly at the way her mind would insist on straying. Private doctors were not her business any more. After tonight she would simply get on with her own life. Then unfortunately her patient took it into his head to tell the nursing supervisor on her early-morning visit that he didn't like a change of nurses. The nursing supervisor's expression didn't brook argument when she said at once that Nurse Challock would be booked to do nights for the whole of his stay. Vivien could scarcely refuse.

She told herself with a shrug that it was only three nights and Caroline's temperature might well not have gone down anyway. Luckily it would still leave Vivien a clear day before she was due to go back to her own proper duties at the hospital. After this, though, she really must remember to write her official letter to the agency!

It was on the third night, when she told herself that she had forgotten him entirely, that she saw Dr Baron again.

It was only for a moment and he was obviously just leaving. He was also deep in conversation with another doctor. They were standing in the corridor as Vivien came along it to the small general kitchen, and she caught sight of a half-turned profile under dark hair, a graceful stance as he listened to what the other man was audibly saying.

'I thought this one might interest you, Justin, that's why I suggested you came in and took a look. How's the new job going? I suppose it must be cutting down on your private patients.'

Vivien couldn't resist taking a swift glance under her lashes as she passed and took a turn round them to go into the kitchen. Unexpectedly her glance was met by light green eyes with a sudden glint of recognition in them. She looked down hastily with a feeling of confusion and scuttled past. She hadn't expected him to remember her. She heard the conversation going on outside and tried to tell herself she wasn't visualising Dr Baron's handsome face as he spoke in that light musical voice.

'. . . Merely a consultancy attachment, but it should prove useful. Oh, by the way, I haven't thanked you for finding me a housekeeper, have I?'

'Oh, Mrs Peters—yes, a nice reliable soul. We had her when my wife was ill. Quite difficult to find good professional service nowadays. Now about this patient of mine. If you want to write him up that's all right with me.'

'Yes, I'll come in and see him again, if you don't mind . . .'

The voices faded along the corridor, lost quickly in its soundproofing. Vivien bit her lip at the way her ears had pricked to listen.

There was no reason why she should be interested in the man. She wasn't. She decided with a touch of acidity that Dr Baron must be helpless as well as rich: why couldn't he look after himself, as a bachelor, instead of needing a housekeeper?

Finding something to criticise about him made her feel abruptly better, but made her give a wry grin at herself too. As she picked up the tray of tea her patient had demanded, and was now allowed provided his fluid intake was carefully measured, she pulled a face at her own idiocy. A handsome young doctor she had worked for *once*, and whom Caroline had already lured into her net: why on earth should she be thinking about him at all!

She got home wearily to find Caroline much better, but since she was reading one of Tom's long letters decided not to distract her by telling her she had missed a sighting of the famous Justin. As Vivien yawned her way to bed she knew that she really would write her signing-off letter to the agency tomorrow. Twelve-hour night shifts when she had just got used to being steadily on days made her feel topsy-turvy.

She didn't remember that the letter was still unwritten until she was arriving for duty two days later and overheard one of the other nurses saying something about 'new rules against moonlighting'. Well, that was all right with her—though it would probably start another union demand for better wages.

Later in the morning she was behind a curtain adjusting a drip for a patient who needed regular transfusions when one of her fellow staff nurses poked her head through.

'Pundit on the ward,' she murmured warningly. 'Thought I'd better tell you because you won't have seen this one—started while you were on days off. Doing some kind of research project, I think.'

Extra pundits were a way of life on the leukaemia unit. 'Thanks,' Vivien said with a smile. 'I'll try not to trip over him. Or her?'

'Him. Trailing a nursing officer and a couple of students.'

'OK. We do get a lot of them, don't we? Shows what a good reputation our unit has!' Vivien turned to smile at her patient as the other nurse disappeared, to include him in their conversation. 'All right, Terry? Quite comfortable? Good, then I'll draw the curtains back so that you don't feel so cut off.'

She swished the print curtains along the rail as she spoke. Then she turned round, and froze.

Pausing to keep out of her way in his swift advance as he approached the next bed, with the nursing officer beside him and two medical students in his wake, was the last person she expected to see. Dr Justin Baron, no less.

Green eyes lighted on her widening ones. Again, as there had been the other night, there was a glint of recognition. His eyes flicked to her name badge, and then to her surprise he stopped to address her.

'Ah, Nurse Challock, so you work here, as well, do you? I didn't know this hospital used agency nurses.'

'Nurse Challock is a staff nurse on this ward,' the

nursing officer put in. Her eyes were suddenly surveying Vivien with far too much alertness.

'Really? Do many people combine the two nowadays? Night duties when you're on a spell of time off, I suppose? You must have a great deal of energy.' He said it pleasantly, nodded to Vivien, and moved on.

His cavalcade moved with him, but from the way the nursing officer glanced at Vivien with a frown and then began to speak quietly to Dr Baron, Vivien could guess with a sinking heart that she was in for a telling off.

All the same, illogically, she was extraordinarily pleased that the 'new job' she had overheard Dr Baron's colleague mention had turned out to be here. She couldn't help thinking involuntarily that his presence on the ward would brighten things considerably. There were advantages to hospital work after all. One just never knew which doctor might turn up in a large, busy, well-known hospital.

CHAPTER TWO

'I'M AFRAID I have no alternative, nurse, but to ask for your immediate resignation.'

Vivien could feel the blood draining out of her cheeks as she stared at the nursing officer across the desk in the latter's small office. 'But Miss Dent——'

'I'm sorry, but you should have thought of the possible consequences before you took on extra duties. Haven't you seen the notice we put up last week? It's quite clearly displayed.' The nursing officer sighed, tapped her pencil, and looked at Vivien with reproof. 'We made a recent decision that we must crack down, as policy. Nurses who are found to be doing agency work in their official time off are to leave. If it weren't for the fact that I've been very pleased with your work since you joined us, it would be dismissal, not resignation! I'm giving you all the latitude I'm allowed.'

'I only—it wasn't regular——'

'Yes, you've explained that you were standing in for a friend in an emergency—but that needed only one night, and you've admitted you did three! You've also told me you "haven't got round to" signing off from the agency's books, and you must allow that that looks suspicious!'

'Honestly Miss Dent, I wasn't going to do it again!'

'Perhaps not, and in your case a warning would have been sufficient. However, a rule is a rule and I can't make any exceptions. I think it's a pity when you're a good nurse.' She looked at Vivien's rebellious face and said drily, 'Would you *like* me to make it dismissal, nurse?'

'No—I——'

'You're given spells of time off because you need them, *not* so that you can earn extra money tiring yourself out. I should have thought someone with your record would have had the sense to see that.' Miss Dent sighed again and looked at Vivien with a touch of exasperation. 'You girls are so silly, and you particularly, when you're doing so well! But there's nothing I can do about it. At least you'll go down as having resigned from your own accord, so that won't look quite so bad on your records. That will be all, nurse, and I'm afraid it's not open to discussion. I shall expect your resignation on my desk today, and you must leave at the end of the week.'

Vivien got up feeling dazed. It was a shattering blow, and as she came out of the office her eyes were stinging with unshed tears. Sacked—even though she had the latitude of writing out her resignation. Sacked from the job she'd entered with so much interest and such high hopes. Just because she'd obliged a friend!

She supposed she should be grateful it wasn't an official dismissal. If it had been, even agency nursing would be closed to her, since all the top agencies were extremely stict about their choice of nurses. And, for the next few months at least, agency nursing looked like Vivien's only choice.

She was suddenly swept by a burning anger towards Dr Justin Baron, since it gave her someone to blame besides herself. It *was* his fault. If he hadn't picked Caroline up in a post office in the first place and caused her to skip a duty, her need to miss another one through illness wouldn't have been a crisis. If he hadn't compounded that by turning up here and giving Vivien away, she would still have a job!

She swept back into the ward feeling angry and sore-hearted and with rage consuming her so much that she felt like walking straight up to him and giving him a piece of her mind. Why had she felt so pleased to see him? He had no business to be here, and it just wasn't fair!

Luckily he had left the ward, but anger and bitterness went on consuming her behind a falsely calm face as she got back to her duties. She was too miserable to say anything to the other nurses, and the knowledge that justice was on the side of the nursing officers didn't help. She hadn't even seen the notice warning of the new rules against moonlighting, but ignorance wasn't counted as an excuse.

Bitterness was still eating her when she came off duty. She walked across the car park in a mixture of brooding rage and misery. It felt as if her entire career had been destroyed—by a chance remark from an unnecessarily handsome doctor, as well as from her own foolishness.

It was unlucky that at just that point Dr Baron came into her view. Several yards away amongst the parked cars she caught sight of a dark head, a graceful cat-like walk, the glimpse of a familiar profile. Reason should have taken her in the other direction as fast as possible. Reason lost. Before she had time to think about it Vivien had swung her steps and was coming up on him fast.

She didn't often lose her temper, but she had to admit that when she did it went off like a rocket. The sight of this man with his hand on the door of a low, smooth black car which was probably a Porsche or something equally elegant fuelled her anger still further, for no good reason. She called out, 'Dr Baron!' and as he turned enquiringly, she brought out between her teeth, 'May I have a word with you?'

'Yes, Nurse Challock?'

'I just wanted to thank you for getting me sacked!'

'I beg your pardon?' Eyebrows snapped down in a frown across the striking light eyes.

'I said, you've just got me sacked! And there was no need for you to tell on me, when I was just standing in for a friend!'

'You've been dismissed for doing agency work on top

of your job? Yes, I can see that they might do that.' He was still frowning. 'But surely if you explained——'

'Oh, I have, but it didn't get me anywhere! And it's *all your fault*!' Vivien brought out furiously, and even angrier because there was something about his smooth handsomeness that sent a tremor through her even now. 'If *you* hadn't——l

'If I hadn't mentioned it no one would have known? True, though I wasn't aware of that at the time. However,' he pointed out, 'you don't seem to be taking into account that you're to blame in the first place, and I've no doubt there's more to this than you're saying. If you're in the habit of doing agency work when you shouldn't, you'd probably have been found out sooner or later.'

His very reasonableness sent Vivient's temper shooting into overdrive. 'I wouldn't,' she snapped, 'because I didn't make a habit of it! You—you just——' The whole thing had started because of a date he had had with Caroline, and at least she could blame him for that. 'It *is* your fault,' she brought out angrily. 'You just swan around doing exactly what you want and other people end up in——'

'I think this conversation's gone on quite long enough.' The tone was sharp enough to act like a douche of cold water. 'For someone who seemed to be a good, or at least an adequate, nurse, you're behaving remarkably like a hysterical child! No, in the circumstances, I will *not* put in a good word for you with the nursing officer. You haven't given me any reason to! I presume that was what you were going to ask me, but the answer's no! And now, good night!'

He opened the car door, slid himself inside, and the door shut with a sharp click behind him. Vivien had to step back quickly as the car's engine started with a deep growl. She was burning and gulping and feeling both foolish and furious. Somehow worst of all was the way he had described her in that dismissive fashion as 'at least an *adequate* nurse'.

It was small comfort that she had made him lose his temper with her, as he obviously had from the way dark brows had snapped down across his eyes in a frown and the mobile mouth had thinned.

She trailed home knowing that she had come off the worse in an encounter which should never have happened. Her rage had died into depression. She hoped beyond hope that Dr Baron wasn't going to appear in her ward during the few days she had left in it.

He looked remarkably young to be a consultant, not more than thirty. Most people were only registrars at that age, but he had 'pundit' status in the hospital. She hadn't yet discovered exactly what research had brought him into the unit on a temporary attachment, but he must be well thought of in the profession . . .

She shook her head sharply to get him out of it and decided defiantly that she would be delighted if she never had to see him again. She couldn't bring herself to mention his name to Caroline, so when she broke her news it was simply to say that her moonlighting had been discovered and its dire consequences.

'Oh, Vivi, no! Look, suppose I go to your nursing officer and explain——'

'It wouldn't do any good. I'm not blaming you, anyway. It was my fault for taking on the extra two nights. It was just—I didn't know about the new ruling——'

'Oh, honey, I'm sorry! Don't cry, lovey, please don't! Look, there's plenty of agency work about, so isn't that at least something? And if you really want a hospital job I'm sure you'll find one again in a few months.'

When Tom rang up later and was told the news he insisted on talking to Vivien and was so full of sympathy that she almost started crying again.

'You're a bloody good nurse, Viv, and don't you forget it,' he said firmly, and sounding forceful rather than helpless. 'Other chances will come, so don't you fret!'

His brotherly affection almost made Vivien cry all over again, and it was a pity his protectiveness merely made her feel wistful.

The rest of the week passed quickly with the occasional flash of anger to enliven it. Anger because Dr Justin Baron turned up in the ward more than once and she felt as if a pair of light green eyes were watching her judicially. They were never actually looking at her if she glanced round, but she was far too aware of him. After making such a fool of herself in front of him, it seemed better to whip herself into a continued rage with him than to feel merely stupid and self-conscious.

Pride had made Vivien tell the other nursing staff simply that she was leaving and going back to agency work because she fancied the variety. It was just as well she'd never signed off with the agency after all, because they seemed to find her availability for duty welcome in the weeks that followed. Vivien resigned herself to going back to waiting for the phone to ring, to accepting bookings for three nights here, two there, a day there, in various nursing homes and clinics.

'There you are, you see, I told you!' said Caroline when they met up after a couple of weeks of merely flying past each other. Unless they were booked in the same nursing home their lives barely seemed to touch. 'You don't mind so much, Vivi, do you? You're even getting asked for by name, so you must be on someone's plus list!'

'Mm, they're doctors I don't remember working for before, but I suppose it shows something or other. I've been wondering whether I wouldn't try to get in somewhere for Stage I Midder, actually.'

'Oh yes, you liked obstetrics during training, didn't you? Only do you really want to go and be a badly-paid trainee midwife somewhere instead of staying here and getting a decent wage? You'd be bound to have to go out of London!' Caroline pulled a dubious face, then added irrelevantly, and wistfully, 'That dishy Justin never did ring me up, and it's weeks since our pub lunch now! I haven't seen hide nor hair of him around the clinics either, have you?'

'No,' Vivien said shortly, feeling thankful that she hadn't. If he still had private patients he certainly wouldn't want to find *her* nursing them, she knew grimly. 'Anyway,' she added lightly but with point, 'didn't you say Tom was planning another visit soon?'

'Mm. Well, never mind.'

During the night duties which came thick and fast over the next days Vivien tried to think sensibly about her future. *Did* she want to go in for midwifery? She had actually delivered a baby once in A and E, though with help from the ambulance crew. However, most of the London teaching hospitals trained only their own people, and Vivien was hardly likely to get in at her own hospital after her recent record. Perhaps she was only feeling restless because agency work rushed her about so much?

She had two nights booked with a Mr Conyngton-Bell, a surgeon who specialised in ear, nose and throat work. He seemed pleased with her care for his patient who had had a laser operation on his pituitry gland through a nasal entry, and said he would like to book her for another patient of his next week and would arrange it through the agency. Vivien agreed meekly, thinking it was all work and would pay the rent.

She got back to the flat after her night duty to find Caroline just getting up. It was an extraordinary sparkly Caroline. She danced through to the kitchen where Vivien was putting the kettle on, and leaned against the door looking like a small tousled child in the cotton-knit nightshirt she was favouring for the chilly early spring.

'You'll never guess what's happened! Justin rang! Just when I'd just about given him up!'

'Oh?' Vivien asked, trying not to show that she had jumped at the name. Her heart had sunk instantly, with a hollow feeling which she put down to a need for breakfast. Justin Baron *again*—as if she hadn't had enough of him!

'He sounded quite odd when I first spoke to him—well, you know how official I can sound when I pick up the phone and say my name! Then I recognised his voice and of course I asked him over. We went out for a drink and then dinner—and oh, Vivi, he's just as gorgeous as ever!'

'Really?'

'Vivi, don't think I'm crazy, but I've fallen for him. He really *is* something. I told him off for not ringing before and he said he must have mislaid my phone number. We had the most marvellous time, he took me to that really swish new place off Knightsbridge. He's so—so—When he looks at me with those extraordinary eyes I just *melt*!'

'What about the fact that Tom's coming to stay again?' asked Vivien, trying not to make it a snap. She was too tired this morning to cope with all this, she decided: it was making her feel, sharply, that Caroline didn't deserve Tom's devotion. '*Tom*. Remember him? The guy you've been going round with for so long?'

'We—ell . . . Actually we've been going off each other for ages. I know it may not have seemed like that, but——'

'No, it hasn't!'

'It's a nice relationship, but it doesn't actually *get* anywhere, you know? And—I can't help it, Vivi, but I really do think I'm in love with Justin. These things do happen fast sometimes!' Caroline peered at Vivien's face, then came out with, 'I don't know why you're looking so angry! Except that I *have* sometimes wondered if you aren't in love with Tom yourself!'

'I'm not!' protested Vivien.

'The way you're always bringing his name up does make me wonder sometimes, that's all.' Caroline's lip jutted mutinously; then before Vivien could say anything she was going on. 'I'm going to have to tell him it's over, so . . . Anyway, please, Vivi, don't criticise, just be happy for me, because Justin's really special—the sort of person one dreams about meeting! If you're so worried about Tom, *you* console him—I've often thought you're really more his type than I am!'

Her words caught Vivien on the raw and made her stiffen. 'I merely like the man enough not to want to see him hurt!' she said stiffly, remembered the old days, and was hard put to it not to give Caroline a really fierce glare. 'But if you really want to replace him with—with someone who's just *smooth*, and probably unprincipled with it, that's you look-out! And now I'm going to bed!'

She swept off to her room without bothering about breakfast and without giving Caroline a chance to reply. It occurred to her as she undressed to get into bed that if Caroline was going to start going around with Justin Baron, no doubt he'd be calling here at the flat. Well, she could only hope he'd be disconcerted to find out who Caroline had as a flatmate . . .

She managed to sleep, which was just as well since she had another duty the following night. When she got up she found Caroline in the sitting-room looking dreamy. Vivien bit back all the comments that came into her mind and made herself smile instead.

'I'm working again tonight, are you?'

'No, luckily, and I had a brilliant idea. You know those theatre tickets I was given! Well, I dug them out and rang Justin to see if he'd like to come. They were for tonight, remember? I said I was asking him as a thank-you for last night's dinner,' Caroline added demurely. 'It's lucky he said where he had his consulting rooms or I wouldn't have known where to reach him, but I did, at lunchtime. He's coming to pick me up at seven-fifteen.'

Her expression was somewhere between triumphant and starry. Vivien's heart sank again and she decided quickly that if he was coming here at seven-fifteen she was going to be out of here at seven-ten at the latest—however much that put her in a rush.

She might have made it if Justin Baron hadn't been early. Presumably he was as eager to see Caroline as she was to see him. Vivien was in uniform and taking a rapid bite at a hastily-assembled sandwich while she strove to pin her hair up with the other hand, when the doorbell rang at exactly seven.

'Oh help, my eye make-up!' shrieked Caroline from her bedroom. 'It'll just have to do!' She emerged looking stunning in cerise, rushed for the door, then stopped and counted three carefully before she opened it.

'Oh, hallo, Justin!'

He came stepping past her with that compact grace, muscular, green-eyed, half-smiling. His clothes looked casual Cardin and the whole effect was quite simply glossy. Vivien, with her mouth full, had the distinct impression that her stomach had dropped away and for a wild moment could visualise the remains of her sandwich falling down through her legs into her feet.

'This is my flatmate Vivien,' said Caroline casually. 'I think I mentioned that she worked for you once, didn't I? I don't expect you remember, though, you must see so many of us!'

'No, I haven't forgotten,' Justin Baron said smoothly. His eyes narrowed almost imperceptibly—like a hunting cat's, Vivien thought wildly—as if he had caught the defensiveness of Vivien's stance. 'Are you on your way to an agency duty, or have you just come back from one?'

'I'm on my way out.' Vivien matched his polite tone, trying not to feel as if her hastily-swallowed sandwich might choke her. The hair she had been trying to pin up chose that moment to slip and cascade down round her shoulders in a dark slippery mass, and she bit her lip in annoyance. 'I've got to get off for a night duty, so if you'll excuse me . . .'

'You're finding plenty of work, I trust?' he asked politely, above Vivien's head because she had had to duck down to look for the grips which had dropped out of her hair. She cast a swift glance up at him, shaking her hair back from her face and longing to give him a glare. He was regarding her with a faintly bored look, one eyebrow raised, and she was irresistibly reminded of his looking down his nose at her in the car park and calling her hysterical.

'Yes, thank you.' She came to her feet and moved to pick up her raincoat, aware that her cheeks had flushed. 'I think my work is proving—*adequate!*'

'I'm sure it is or I should have heard. Most of the doctors who use the private clinics know each other.' For a horrified second she fancied a threat in that, but he was going on smoothly, 'I'm glad you're finding agency work full-time suits you. You and Caroline both work for the same agency, I gather. Have you known each other long?'

'Practically for ever. We trained together and Vivi's my closest friend.' Caroline didn't seem to sense the undercurrents, though to Vivien they were so thick in the air that they could have been cut with a blunt knife. 'Are you off then, lovey? Have a good night!'

Vivien was only too glad of an excuse to go. She decided to put her hair up on the bus and was out of the door as fast as her legs would take her. She was *not* going to spend her evening, either, thinking about Caroline and Justin Baron at the theatre, or going for a drink afterwards, or any of the other things they might be doing. Definitely not.

There were no sounds or movements from Caroline's

room when Vivien arrived back at the flat in the morning, but she must have come in as her evening bag was flung down on the table and her kicked-off sandals lay in one corner of the sitting room. For a moment as Vivien put her key in the lock she had wondered what she would do if she found Justin Baron's jacket lying obviously in the sitting-room too—but there had been no smooth car parked outside, merely the usual collection of old bangers. He probably wasn't the type to stay over in a shabby multi-tenanted flat. No doubt, Vivien thought sarcastically, the presence of his housekeeper had stopped him sweeping Caroline off to *his* place.

When the telephone rang she moved to it quickly before it could wake Caroline and probably bring on a starry-eyed description of last night's entertainments. The call was for Caroline, a booking for the next two nights. Vivien wrote it out clearly and propped it up where her friend would see it. Then she went wearily back to her tea and toast, and took them to bed with her.

At five o'clock that afternoon she was answering the phone again, since Caroline had raced out to buy spare tights before her evening's duty. Vivien herself was free for once. She lifted the receiver and a brisk female voice said, 'Miss Challock??'

'Yes, speaking?'

'This is Dr Baron's secretary. Would you please hold on, I'll put you through.'

The efficient voice had gone away before Vivien could snap that the call must be for someone else. Wariness caught at her abruptly as she realised she had been addressed by name. Before she had time to do more than stiffen a smooth and recognisable voice spoke in her ear.

'Good afternoon, Miss Challock. I'm glad I've caught you. Are you booked up for the next few days?'

'No, I—Why?'

'You come straight to the point, don't you? There's a patient I'd like you to take on for me, if you will. Could you start tomorrow morning, and arrange to be available for—oh, at least four days, and possibly longer?'

'I could. But——'

'I'll arrange the booking through your agency, naturally, but I just wanted to check that you'd be free. The patient's a ten-year-old child, Philip Mantagna, and he needs to be privately nursed while he's undergoing tests for glandular fever. The place is——'

'Wait a minute, Dr Baron.' Vivien was trying to pull herself together out of sheer surprise. 'Why do you want *me*?' she asked bluntly.

'I've seen you work with children before you gave up your recent ward-work, and you seemed capable and suitably calm. I also need someone in a hurry. Do you have objections?'

'No . . . But Caroline's the one who usually specialises in children. She may not have mentioned that to you.'

'I don't usually mix social and professional matters,' he said, sounding bored about it. The words, as well as the tone of his voice, stung. 'Do you want this job, Nurse Challock, or not? Because if not, please don't waste my time!'

'Yes, I'll take it.' At least she could prove to him that she was good at her job. 'Please will you tell me where you want me to report for duty tomorrow, and what time?'

'Eight a.m. at the Harraday Clinic in Cranshaw Street. The boy's going in this evening, so you'll take over from the night staff. You'll find a Dr Asscher in charge since Dr Harraday's away at the moment. They're currently short-staffed, so I said I'd find my own agency nurse. I'll expect you to be there tomorrow, then.'

There was a click and he had rung off. No polite chitchat; just the offer of a job and some terse information.

A job—from *him* of all people.

CHAPTER THREE

PHILIP MANTAGNA was small, skinny and fractious. Boot-button brown eyes glared at Vivien above his top sheet and he greeted her with the information that his bed was lumpy and he wanted his mother. Vivien already knew from the night staff that his mother was abroad and he had been brought in by an uncle who was apparently in charge of him. She ignored his hostility and smiled at him.

'You look too grown up to need your mother for a mild fever. Show me where the lumps are in your bed and I'll smooth them out—that's what I'm here for. Do you like to be called Philip in full, or something for short?'

'Philip,' he said inimically.

'OK, Philip. See if you can guess what *my* name is. Bet you can't. It begins with a V, see, here on my label? I've never yet met anyone who can get it right first time, so I'll give you, let's see, three guesses. If you don't hit then it'll stay a secret!'

'That's not fair.' He stuck his lower lip out mutinously, but it had got his mind temporarily off his unhappiness, which was what Vivien had intended. Her quiet and calmly practical voice seemed to have a good effect on him too.

The Harraday Clinic specialised in children and was very well organised. Small single rooms ran the length of the corridor with a convalescent children's play area at the end of it. Everywhere was well soundproofed and nurses moved around quietly under the charge of a blue-uniformed Sister. There seemed to be a generally friendly atmosphere, and bright curtains with clowns on them hung at Philip's window. All the same Vivien could feel sympathy with a small boy feeling ill in a strange place amongst strangers, and she set herself to coax him gently into feeling more settled.

By mid-morning she felt she was winning over young Philip's automatic hostility. She had seen from his notes on their clip outside his door that he was an only child and guessed he was used to a lot of attention. He had softened enough to cling to her hand when Dr Asscher, thirty-fiveish and kind and pleasant, came to take a blood sample for testing. Dr Asscher obviously had children of his own, and between them he and Vivien managed to make the blood test a matter of interest rather than something to fear.

Memories of her former ward, and what she had now heard was Justin Baron's specialty—generalised cancers—set her wondering with concern whether her young patient was being tested for rather more than glandular fever. She pushed that into the back of her mind with a sharp hope that it wasn't so, and set herself to entertain Philip with a discussion of his favourite television series. She was still in the middle of that when the door opened behind her and a glance round showed Justin Baron himself.

Philip shot up in bed with his expression a mixture of mutiny and entreaty and his voice going up into a squeak. 'Uncle Justin, Uncle Justin, have you come to take me home again? I don't have to stay here, do I?'

It was like looking at a different man to see the green eyes alight with affection as Justin Baron moved quickly to field one small boy trying to scramble out of bed into his arms. 'Don't be silly, PJ,' he said with gentle reproof, and gave Philip a reassuring hug before depositing him back against his pillows. 'If you've got to be ill in bed you're far better off here than moping in my flat, now aren't you?'

'Yes, but——'

'I've just looked in to see how you are, and I can't stay long, mind!' He seated himself on the side of the bed. 'If you're going to bounce around your nurse will banish me, uncle or no—you're supposed to be resting!'

'She can't, she couldn't tell *you* what to do. She's paid to look after me, so she's got to do what *I* tell her too!'

'Oh no, PJ. *You* do what *she* tells you.' There was a note in the light voice that brooked no argument, and Justin Baron glanced round to acknowledge Vivien for the first time. She was still feeling stunned by the fact that he had booked her to look after his own nephew —wonders would never cease! 'I'm going to give her instructions to tell me exactly how you behave, too,' Justin added warningly as the boy's face began to take on its mutinous look again. 'I'm acting as your guardian, remember? And who's the only member of the family you can't get round?'

'You are,' a small sulky voice said into a waiting silence, and then on a wobble, 'but I don't like your sending me away because I'm ill, and Mrs Peters could have looked after me.'

'Not in this case. She was there to see to you when you came in from school and when I had to be out working, but her job's housekeeping, not nursing!'

'Well—well, Dolores then! She never minds being with me——'

'Dolores has other things to do than mind you full-time,' his uncle said unsympathetically. Vivien thought he could have sounded kinder. She also wondered who Dolores might be. 'She has her own job to do, so you wouldn't really expect her to stay in the flat and nurse you, would you? I'm sorry, feller, but I did warn you when you came to stay with me that you mustn't expect to monopolise everyone's time!'

It flitted through Vivien's mind that he seemed an unlikely person to be left in charge of a child, in spite of the obvious affection with which he had greeted Philip.

She almost jumped as he glanced round again, and smiled directly at her in a way which involuntarily made her aware of his charm.

'Do you think you could rustle me up a cup of coffee from somewhere? Meantime I'm going to show PJ that I'm not quite the wicked uncle he thinks me by demonstrating the game I've brought him!'

The words sent Philip bouncing back into good temper and he was being amiably allowed to search his uncle's pockets as Vivien slipped out of the room. She hoped abruptly that she *hadn't* been booked to look after Philip because of her leukaemia experience. That would be a bitter irony, for Justin Baron.

She found she was wondering who Dolores might be. She sounded suspiciously like a live-in girlfriend—but not one he was faithful to, if he was taking Caroline out. It could sound a lot like double-dealing that he had simply said he 'wasn't married'.

She went thoughtfully back into her patient's room to find uncle and nephew amiably absorbed in a small dice game set out on the counterpane. It seemed to be something to do with footballers scoring goals. Vivien couldn't help being amused by the sight of the sophisticated doctor occupied with such apparent absorption in a childish game. As she set the tray down he was saying with satisfaction,

'There you are, I'm catching up, that's Mosta one, Sliema two! I'm still not sure I won't disallow your second goal, though!'

'I didn't cheat, and Sliema always wins!'

'All right!' A hand ruffled the child's hair amiably. Justin sat up, his eyes going ruefully to Vivien's watching face. 'He's as mad about football as all the Maltese,' he said on a chuckle. 'Ah, my coffee, thank you. No, I'll take it black. I think we've played enough for now, PJ, though I expect you can persuade your nurse to play it with you later! Time for you to have a rest.'

Philip settled back obediently on his pillows, though Vivien thought he shot her an odd little look of triumph as he did so. The alternating lassitude and fever he had been showing did *seem* characteristic of glandular fever.

Justin was packing the football game back into its small box, then chatting gently to his nephew as he finished his coffee. It struck Vivien again that this was a different man from the smooth and glamorous private doctor—and certainly different, and much more human, than the sarcastic man she had shouted at in the car park. She wished she didn't have to remember that.

'A word with you before I go——'

He had stood up and as he moved towards the door a small gesture summoned Vivien with him.

'Uncle Justin? You promise you'll ask Dolores if she *will* come and see me?'

'Yes, I'll ask her. She'll probably come in with me some time. I *almost* think she's quite fond of you,' Justin Baron said teasingly, but added, 'You must remember, though, that she's busy, and she can't come in here and read to you as she did at home. I expect you'll find the nurses here are just as good at that. Particularly this one—after all, I did choose her particularly for you!'

Vivien might have felt flattered by that if she hadn't known it was simply designed to see that her charge did what she told him. She felt a tinge of colour come up into her cheeks just the same and was glad she had turned her back on the doctor to open the door.

Outside, she waited obediently for whatever instructions he had called her out to give.

'You've probably gathered that my nephew's a bit of a handful. My sister spoiled him, probably due to being widowed so early.' He said the words without preamble. 'It's a pity in a sense that he has to be ill away from home, though on the other hand if his mother were here she'd be panicking and encouraging him to feel worse.

The tests should tell us whether I'm right about his symptoms.'

'Glandular fever *is* the probable diagnosis?'

'I don't plan to leap to any other conclusions. My sister certainly would, hence my decision not to contact her for the moment. PJ's been staying with me because it was felt he needed a man in charge of him. It's the first time I've been settled enough to help out.' He spoke shortly, and not as if he was aware of telling Vivien more than she had asked. He frowned for a moment. 'By the way, wasn't that unnecessarily formal of you to refuse to give him your first name?'

'It was only to distract him by making him guess!'

'Oh. Well, I've given you away, so please look suitably surprised when he comes up with the right answer. By the way, your agency seems to think you're half promised to someone later in the week. I trust it won't matter if that's cancelled?'

'It was only something tentative, a Mr Conyngton-Bell whose patient I was nursing said something about booking me again. It wasn't definite.'

'Oh yes, well, since I recommended you to him I can square that.'

'*You* did?' she echoed.

'There's no need to look so surprised. I seem to remember you did suggest I owed you something.' He spoke drily, one eyebrow going up. 'As to the present, though . . . I've seen you work, as I said, and it occurred to me that the kind of calm you show on duty might be to PJ's advantage.'

His words made Vivien feel about an inch high. She certainly hadn't imagined he could have been recommending her to his fellow doctors. 'Th-thank you,' she brought out. 'There was something I wanted to ask you—is your nephew always called PJ?'

'No, the only person who calls him that is me. He's Philip Justin, so it's a kind of home joke between us.' He gave a sudden wry smile with a glance towards the nearest window. 'Home would be somewhere warmer than this, since Malta's spring temperature is a great deal more clement than England's. That's why I thought at first he was simply getting recurrent chills. I'm not used to having to be a parent, so I hope it isn't going to be a case of "coblers' children".'

He walked away abruptly and Vivien knew he had betrayed a worry he didn't want to state any more openly. Sometimes it was worse to know too much than too little . . . and she couldn't help her heart going out to him in the fervent hope that his diagnosis would prove to be the right one.

She went back into Philip's room looking deliberately cheerful and found him resting obediently. He gave her another of those slyly triumphant looks out of half-closed eyes and she wondered with amusement when he would come out with his correct guess at her name.

He was a funny child, sometimes quite babyish, at others sharp enough to suit his age. She wouldn't have guessed, looking at him, the relationship between him and Justin Baron. It was difficult not to speculate about this family with its mixed Maltese and English background. Was Malta usually 'home' to Justin Baron too?

After she had been out to lunch she and Philip played the fooball game again as he demanded. He didn't seem seriously ill, which was a relief, even if it made her job more nannying than nursing. He told her in a lordly fashion which Maltese football team was which and why he supported Sliema even though he lived in Valletta, and gave her the names of various places and footballers which varied from the normal to the unpronounceable. When Vivien saw him getting flushed and droopy again she gathered the dice and counters firmly together.

'I think we'll stop for a while. You didn't eat any lunch, did you? Do you want anything now? I could heat you up some soup—no? All right then, have another drink of squash to cool you down. And if you'll lie quiet I *might* let you have the television on later.'

'Is it *He-Man* today?'

'No, 'fraid not, only *Tom and Jerry*,' Vivien told him, consulting the television paper which someone had thoughtfully provided.

'That's the one Dolores likes best. Except she's sorry for the cat. Uncle Justin calls her Dolly,' added Philip, looking suddenly fretful, 'but I'm not allowed to!'

'Perhaps she doesn't really like people shortening her name—particularly when it's a rather beautiful one.'

'She doesn't mind when *he* does. I like Dolores, even if she does cook funny-tasting things for us when Mrs Peters is off. I'm going to have my third guess about *your* name,' Philip added, switching subjects abruptly and gazing up guilelessly with his boot-button eyes. 'It's —Vivien!'

'Brilliant, you've got it! There now, most people say Victoria, Valerie, Vera. You're cleverer than I thought!'

'Uncle Justin says it's usually a man's name. I told him that was what I was going to guess,' Philip added hastily, with a look that defied her to doubt him.

'Well, he's wrong,' said Vivien, 'it's only a man's name when it's spelt with an a. Actually I *was* named after an uncle, spelt the other way. I don't suppose your Uncle Justin knows how I spelt it.'

'Yes, he does, he spelled it for me. After I told him my guess!'

'Oh. Well, I'm—I'm surprised. And if he asks you can tell him there was a famous Welsh witch called Vivien, and see what he says about that!'

'Are you a witch? Can you do spells?'

'No, silly! I don't come from Wales, either. My father's a farmer in Devon and I've got lots and lots of older brothers. There now, I think we've had enough of names. I'm just going to take your pulse.'

'*My* father was a Member of Parliament,' Philip

announced loftily, wriggling as Vivien tried to still his wrist. 'He was killed in a water-skiing accident. His name was Lewis. Lewis Mantagna, of course, everyone at home's heard of him.' That seemed to matter to him much more than the fact that his father had been killed, an announcement he made in a purely practical voice. Vivien supposed it must have happened when he was too young to remember. 'Uncle Justin's the only doctor in our family. I might be a doctor too, or a footballer. Grandma says we don't have footballers in our kind of family. Grandma's got a house on Gozo, but she isn't there at the moment because she's going to see Aunt Louisa in America. She brought me to Uncle Justin on the way. Grandma says——'

'Philip, will you please keep still? And I think you're chattering too much!'

'Don't you want to hear what Grandma said to Uncle Justin? She told him he ought to get married and he was getting spoilt. And thirty's too old to keep on flying about. That's because he flew out to Saudi Arabia again, I expect. He went to see a patient, one from when he was working there.'

'Really?' asked Vivien, fascinated by this flood of information. The thought of Justin Baron being lectured by his mother on being spoilt was irresistible.

'I asked Dolores if she thought Uncle Justin ought to get married, but she only laughed. She told him what I said too and he said "Only if you'll have me" and then they both laughed. I wish people wouldn't have jokes when I don't know why,' Philip added, looking suddenly all prepared to get in a rage about it. Vivien hastily selected a book from his locker and set about reading to him in her calmest voice. It had been on the tip of her tongue to say something that would lead him on to say more, until it occurred to her guiltily that pumping a child was *not* good nursing behaviour.

Philip relayed as his first news the next morning that

Dolores had come in with Uncle Justin to visit him after Vivien had left. He proudly displayed the new book she had brought him. The small boy was feeling distinctly better today, though since that made him bored it didn't make him any easier to handle. There was a minor tantrum because he wasn't to get out of bed and run about, and a rather long sulk afterwards. When Dr Asscher did his rounds he raised a sympathetic eyebrow at Vivien. Of Justin, today, there was no sign.

Philip's improvement didn't last and his temperature went up and down with monotonous regularity over the next few days. The blood tests had apparently been inconclusive, and Vivien tried to remind herself that the glandular fever virus was notoriously difficult to pin down. She was able to see Justin's patience and concern and was touched by the gentleness he showed as he made time to come in and sit with Philip to reassure the small boy with his familiar presence. It began to be quite genuine to say, 'Look, here's Uncle Justin, that's nice, isn't it?'—and to smile at him encouragingly when he had to leave too, in a collusion of cheerfulness which would let him see just the same that she knew how he must be feeling.

'I wish we could track this thing down——' They were outside Philip's door again, where she had gone on the excuse of seeing him out. He ran a hand through his hair, his eyes narrowed in exasperation. 'It doesn't *look* like anything else but the damned infective mononucleosis bug, except that he's rather young for the usual age to get it—but I wish I knew if there's anything I've left out.'

'I'm sure there isn't. Anyway, you've got this other paediatrician coming to see him, haven't you?'

'Yes, I'm just waiting for him to be free. I could wish Harraday wasn't away just now—everyone says he's the best diagnostician where children are concerned.' Justin glanced at her and a smile lit his face. 'You're good with the boy, and thanks, I know he isn't easy——'

'Easy to get fond of,' Vivien assured him, feeling a glow of pleasure for the compliment. 'He's quite the comic in his better moods, you know!'

'Yes, I know, even if he'd try the patience of a saint at other times. You won't mind that I've made it an indefinite booking with your agency, then?'

'Not at all. I—I'm glad that——'

'So am I. Well, I must go. I seem to be living by snatched moments at the present.' He gave her an oddly intent look, another smile, and then he was walking away down the corridor. Vivien watched him go. It was hard suddenly to remember that she'd ever felt a grudge against him . . .

She hadn't seen Caroline for days: their hours simply hadn't co-ordinated. She did see her just over a day later, though; she came in early from a night duty just as Vivien was getting up, and slumped down to pour herself a mug of tea from Vivien's breakfast pot.

'I've had so many night duties on the trot lately that it's just too much! Time I had a break. I haven't even had the chance to see Justin! Are you still on his patient?'

'Yes . . .'

'Lucky old you. I s'pose it's because you took one for him before. But listen, don't you dare poach——' Caroline caught herself up quickly. 'Only joking, I know you wouldn't, when you know I'm batty about the man! I *must* get some time off so that we can get together again! Ouf, I'm tired, I don't think I can manage anything else except this tea, and I'm going to take that to bed with me!'

She wandered away before Vivien could snap, 'You'd better ask him about someone called Dolores!'—and even then she didn't know why she should want to sound so tart about it. Justin Baron's private life was nothing to do with her and it wasn't really up to her to go round delivering warnings either. Besides, she hadn't actually mentioned to Caroline that it was Justin's nephew she was nursing as well as his patient: she hadn't had the chance or felt the inclination to discuss it. She shrugged with a sudden and incomprehensible fit of bad temper and went to get ready for work.

Philip had had a better night, but was whiny. After a morning that required all her skilful tact to calm him Vivien went out to lunch, deciding wryly that it might have been better to send for his mother after all, because he had suddenly gone into a homesick fit and was moping for her. Justin's determination not to send for her suddenly seemed rather autocratic. Vivien walked down the clinic steps wondering whether she dared raise that point with him—and then suddenly she found her arm being caught in a strong grip.

'Viv?'

The tall shape she had almost walked into reformed itself from a blur and turned into Tom Ainslie. Vivien's jaw dropped.

'*Tom?* What on earth are you doing here?'

He kept hold of her arm and almost marched her off along the pavement. Looking up at him, Vivien saw he was wearing a haggard expression.

'I didn't want to go to the flat, so I rang the agency and said I was a doctor and asked where you were working at the moment.' His voice was jerky. 'Some sort of receptionist inside said you'd be free for lunch, so I hung about. Viv, what *is* all this about Caroline? Who is this—this man she's madly in love with?'

Vivien's heart sank abruptly. She shouldn't have forgotten him. She practically had. 'Hold hard, Tom,' she said quickly. 'It's Caroline you ought to go and talk to, not me.'

'If anyone knows what's been going on, it's you. Is she serious? Or is it just something I've done?'

'Oh dear. Look, I'm sorry——'

'What has she actually said? To you?'

'Well, she . . . she said the two of you had been going off each other . . .'

'*Did* she?' The expression on Tom's face was bleak and Vivien's heart was squeezed with sympathy. 'She might have told *me*,' he said bitterly.

Vivien was suddenly furious with Caroline. And with Justin Baron, the cause of all this. 'Look,' she said helplessly, 'I don't really know what—I mean, I suppose she wrote to you—There *is* this man she's met, but it's quite a new thing and it may—may just have turned her head for the moment——'

'Show me my rival and I'll knock his bloody head off!'

'That won't help,' Vivien told him hastily. She had a sudden vision of Tom taking a swing at Justin and for a moment it was tempting to think it would serve him right. 'You'd do better to—to wait it out,' she went on with a quiver in her voice, thinking that there was always Dolores.

'I'm not sure that I want to, not now. She's done the switch too abruptly. I thought we both knew where we stood. But one minute everything's roses, the next—' Tom broke off, his jaw grim. 'Maybe it *is* time to call a halt!'

'Oh, Tom, I'm so sorry!'

'You know something?' He was looking down at her and suddenly the grey eyes were filled with appreciation. 'You're worth twice as much as she is—you needn't think I haven't noticed. If it hadn't been for——'

'Don't,' Vivien said swiftly, feeling confused, hot suddenly, and defensive. If he had looked at her like that a year ago . . . 'You're just looking for consolation, and that never really works, you know it doesn't!'

'I don't know about that. You and I go back a long way. Caroline's a kind of illness, I'll admit that, and I'm beginning to wish I'd never caught it! All right,' he added quickly, 'I know it's probably the wrong moment, but don't write it off, Viv. Now, we seem to be walking in some direction or other, and is it towards your lunch? How about having it with me—and on me?'

'Tell me what you're doing down from Edinburgh. You haven't run out on the job?' asked Vivien with sudden anxiety.

'No, I'd arranged to come down again, remember? I do seem to be rather easily forgettable!'

His mouth had twisted in bitterness. 'No, you're not,' Vivien said swiftly. 'All right, let's go and have lunch —but I've only got an hour, and then I've got to get back to an extremely recalcitrant patient!'

She expected to spend lunch listening to him sympathetically, but he refused to let Caroline's name be brought into the conversation at all. They discussed his work in Edinburgh instead. His locum was due to finish in less than two months now, but he wanted to find another one: he had always wanted to be a GP but had to save up to buy into a partnership.

'I've been thinking of going in for Stage I Midwifery,' Vivien offered, 'but I haven't got very far because I don't know where I'd train.'

'Try the Midlands. There are usually locums going there too . . .' He gave her a hopeful look. 'We could try for something in the same place? Come out with me tonight and we'll talk about it some more. I've booked into the YMCA. What time are you off?'

Vivien hesitated, but he was looking at her pleadingly. She couldn't help thinking how depressed he would get on his own. 'All right, then. It'll have to be lateish. I'll meet you at . . . nine at Oxford Circus? And I'd better be getting back now. Oh help, is that the time? I must run!'

Tom walked back with her, his long legs easily keeping up with her fast pace. They reached the Harraday Clinic and just as Vivien was about to smile a goodbye at him Tom caught hold of her and practically lifted her off her feet.

His mouth found hers in an unexpectedly long and comprehensive kiss. Vivien felt slightly dizzy from his ardour and tried to tell herself that she had only kissed him back because he had caught her by surprise. She disentangled herself, gazing up at him breathlessly.

Then she discovered that someone else had walked round them and was standing now with the door half open, looking back at her with a cool green-eyed stare.

'You're coming in, Nurse Challock?'

Justin Baron glanced at his watch deliberately as he spoke. He sounded unnecessarily frosty. Vivien was suddenly back with remembering all sorts of reasons why she might dislike him; though uppermost was the one that he had no need to look through her like that just because she was one minute late.

And if he did but know it, only the fact that Tom didn't know who he was was saving him from the fierce swing of an Edinburgh fist. Vivien put her chin up and marched past him with a look as cold as his own.

She was sure he looked back at Tom with a small frown. Her heart gave a jerk and she was suddenly wondering what his thoughtful expression meant. He couldn't ever have seen Tom with Caroline, surely?

It seemed unlikely. All the same, she could have sworn there was *something* behind that slight narrowing of his eyes.

CHAPTER FOUR

JUSTIN didn't stay long and Vivien managed to keep out of his way until he left. She certainly wasn't in any mood to exchange pleasantries with him just now. His presence had made Philip even more restless for once, too. That didn't help either, and made the rest of her duty seem long.

She spent an evening with Tom when he was as affectionate as she would allow him to be, and seemed determined to behave as if Caroline didn't exist. It was almost easy to join in the pretence that they had gone back to the beginning again. When he kissed her good night at the nearest Underground station to the flat there seemed to be a lot to be said for snuggling together to keep warm.

'Spring's the season of change,' Tom murmured, 'and I'm very glad about it. Darling Viv, you really are very special, you know that?' His lips brushed her forehead. 'It's a pity I have to go back tomorrow, now that I've found you properly . . .'

'Seriously, I ought to tell Caroline you were down——'

'Who?' He wrapped her even more tightly into his arms, his voice stubborn. 'Don't tell anybody anything. It's not important any more. I'm glad we discovered that disco—I love the way your hair flies out around you while you're dancing . . .'

He kissed her in such an amorous fashion that it blotted out thought. It was a pity that Vivien had to surface to an immediate memory of someone else's words on the subject of her hair. Philip had informed his uncle importantly that his nurse was named after a witch; Justin had studied her consideringly and agreed with great solemnity that very long dark hair and dark blue eyes might well be the sign of a witch, so they had all better be careful. Remembering that, just now, was an irritant and made Vivien stir sharply in Tom's arms.

'I've got to let you go, I suppose,' he said on a sigh, sounding regretful. 'Listen, I'll write to you. Think about the idea of doing your midder, and we'll see if we can land up in the same place.'

He sounded so determined about that that Vivien felt dizzy. Life had suddenly got shaken up with a vengeance! As she walked away from Tom she felt an unwary stab of guilt. Still, it wasn't *her* fault that Caroline and Tom had broken up . . .

She felt unusually moody as she made her way in to work the next morning without having seen her flatmate, and was unusually glad that she hadn't, when Caroline's greeting would undoubtedly have been something about Justin and Vivien was still feeling confused over Tom. It didn't help to find Philip both fractious and feverish and in one of his insecure, clinging states. It helped even less when Justin came in in the middle of the morning and discussed things over the small boy's head.

'Uncle Justin, I don't want to see a *nuther* doctor——'

'Don't be silly, PJ, and don't interrupt. Lie still and don't fuss. As I was saying——'

It was unusual of him to be so short with the boy, but even if it was worry which was causing it, Vivien thought with irritation that he ought to be able to see how particularly nervy Philip was today. She cast him a darkling glance with all her resentment from yesterday in it, deciding that if *she* knew how much Philip hated people talking across him, *he* ought to know it even more. When he left, glancing at his watch as if he was in a hurry, she wasn't at all surprised when Philip promptly burst into tears.

The afternoon and evening were spent keeping Philip

calm, but when the time came for Vivien to go off duty he was suddenly hysterical. Dr Asscher had to prescribe a sedative for him, and Vivien set about being her most soothing.

'It's all right, I promise I won't go away until you've dropped off to sleep. Look, I'm going to sit right here beside you and read to you. Then you can shut your eyes and you'll *know* I'm still here, won't you?'

She was still there at half-past eight but was congratulating herself that Philip's eyelids were drooping and his tight clutch on her hand was lessening. When the door opened she glanced round warningly to make a hushing sign, then saw it was Justin coming in. Philip's heavy eyelids promptly flew up.

'Uncle Justin——'

'There now, here's your uncle come to say good night to you and then you can go to sleep properly.' Vivien tried not to sound stiff, though she felt inclined to tell the doctor with unsuitable sharpness that he should try not to upset his nephew further. She pulled her hand away from Philip's and smiled down at him with deliberate reassurance. 'I'm not going away just yet, I'm going to tidy up in here first.'

She didn't look at Justin as she moved to let him take her place beside the bed. A moment later she was surprised to hear Philip break into a foreign language which she presumed must be Maltese, though she had never heard him speaking anything but English before.

From the way he kept glancing at her and then muttering earnestly to his uncle, she must be the subject of the conversation. She felt abruptly self-conscious, but she was also straining her ears in unconscious fascination to hear how Justin would sound if he answered in the same language. However, he ran an affectionate hand through the child's curly hair and answered in English.

'It's not polite to talk secrets in a language someone else can't understand. Besides, I'm out of practice, I've been more used to speaking straight Arabic. Well, all right.' He said something swift and incomprehensible, bent his head to kiss the child, and stood up.

'Don't worry, I'll sort it out. Good night, sleep well, don't dream of lions!'

This extraordinary pronouncement must be something Philip was used to, as he shut his eyes obediently. Vivien came to herself abruptly and stiffened as Justin came towards her. As he opened the door for her to precede him out of the room she glanced pointedly at her watch, then wished she hadn't as it reminded her of his making the same gesture at lunchtime yesterday. The memory brought the colour up into her cheeks and made her face him resentfully in the quiet corridor.

'You're late off, so I'll drive you home,' he told her.

'It's all right, thank you. There's no need——'

'Do as you're told, for heaven's sake! I want to talk to you about PJ. Get your coat and I'll meet you in the hall.'

It wasn't until Vivien was walking away from him that she realised she could have told him to say whatever he had to say here. She slid into her navy raincoat feeling uncertain. When she came out into the hall she was by the door looking smooth and blank.

He ushered her out to the low black car, which he had parked right outside on a double yellow line. Anyone else would have got a parking ticket, Vivien thought resentfully, making her thoughts deliberately nasty because she was reminded of the last time he had offered her a lift. He opened the car door for her to get in, and she was far too aware of the closeness of one muscular shoulder beside her as he settled into his seat. He didn't speak until they were moving and the powerful engine had settled to a deep purr.

'PJ tells me you're angry with me for upsetting him.' The words came coolly across the small space between them. 'He says he can tell because your eyes go "all dark and funny" when you look at me. He's an insecure child at the moment, so you might bear that in mind—particularly since this other paediatrician is coming in to see him tomorrow evening!'

'He is? Oh, good——' The words came out involuntarily, but then Vivien rallied to find an answer to his accusation. 'You did upset him,' she retorted stiffly, 'you know he hates people talking over his head, and——'

'I told you, I'm not used to being a parent. We both know he's an over-protected only child, and that makes things more difficult. Have you got any more criticisms you'd like to make?'

The sarcasm in his voice made Vivien able to think of several, but since they were none of them anything to do with Philip she restrained herself. His tone suggested that it wasn't a nurse's place to criticise him, too, and she was opening her mouth on a reluctant apology when he spoke again, glancing across at her with a suddenly satirical twist to his mouth.

'Nice try, but it won't wash! You were bristling at me yesterday as well as today, and you know it! Are you really so sensitive at being caught in a clinch on the clinic doorstep? And who is he, anyway—this blond giant who gives me the feeling I've seen him somewhere before?'

'A doctor,' Vivien said frostily. 'And I really don't see that it's any of your business——'

'No? It certainly is when it affects your behaviour towards my patient!'

'It didn't!' She made the retort indignantly. 'I haven't been in the least different towards Philip! And that reminds me——'

'Don't change the subject. We were talking about your private life——'

'Well, don't! It certainly isn't your business, since I only work for you. I don't ask about *your* private life, though goodness knows I get it thrown down my throat enough! Oh—oh, we're here, this is our street!'

'So it is, and you don't need to direct me, I know which house, remember? That's an interesting comment you've just made,' added Justin, not slowing down, 'and in such a sharp voice you'd think I was Bluebeard at least!'

'You've gone past——'

'I know. I think I'll drive round the block. Then you can tell me exactly what you meant!'

'Merely that I share a flat with your—your current girlfriend.' Anger was suddenly sparking in her on Tom's behalf and making her forget caution. 'At least that's what she seems to be, though I assume you don't want her to find out about Dolores——'

It came out without Vivien meaning it to and simply because she needed to find a sarcasm to match the sardonic note which had been there in his voice. She went on quickly, 'She does come into Philip's conversation a lot, it would occur to anyone to wonder. And since you did ask——'

'Well, so my cover's blown, is it? I should have thought of that. And like a good little friend you're being protective towards Caroline?'

They were coming round to the flat again. To Vivien's surprise he suddenly speeded up and they shot past, swung sharply round the next corner, roared on to the next and shot across some traffic lights on amber. Vivien was almost flung against him and would have been if it hadn't been for the seat-belt holding her in place. 'Hold tight,' Justin's voice said coolly, 'and pray for a lack of police cars!'

'Where are we going——?'

'Who knows? I just get tired of playing the upper-echelon sobersides all the time!'

Vivien gritted her teeth as he flung the car round another corner. 'Malta's full of hairpin bends,' he said above the growl of the engine, 'usually on one-in-four hills, so that is nothing on level ground! Don't you like going fast? I do, given half a chance!'

'I *don't*, given the city accident rates!'

'Oh, these side streets are nice and clear, don't you think?'

Justin swung round into a quiet square and abruptly pulled up. His fit of irresponsibility seemed to have enlivened him and his eyes were gleaming as he turned to look at her. Light eyes, made grey by the street lighting that filtered into the car, and filled with a devilish amusement that curled his mouth into its dangerous smile.

'You're full of surprises, Vivien the witch,' he said smoothly. 'Now, are you going to tell me it takes more than being kidnapped unexpectedly to put you off your stroke?'

'It does, and have you kidnapped me? If so I can't think why. I *thought* you said you wanted to talk to me about Philip?'

'I do. Don't carry your quarrels to work with you: it worries him if he thinks you dislike me. He told me you had a wide smiley mouth and he liked you so I wasn't to let you go away.' His intent gaze sent a shiver through her and she was overwhelmingly aware of his closeness in the interior of the small car. 'He's right,' Justin went on consideringly, 'you do have a wide mouth. That's usually supposed to denote generosity and good temper, isn't it? It's also extraordinarily tempting . . .'

For a mesmerising moment Vivien was sure he was going to lean forward and kiss her. Her breath seemed to catch in her throat. There was a yearning temptation to sit still and let it happen. Then she was saying, in an angry rush,

'If you think you're going to add me to your list of——'

'No, because I promised PJ I'd make things up with

you. And that doesn't seem exactly the way to do it, in the circumstances. Pity!'

He pulled away from the kerb as he spoke, not fast this time but quite decorously. Vivien wanted to choke at the sheer nerve of him—sounding as if he could add her to his collection if he only cared to try! She was aware all the same of a sharp feeling of regret, and that was extremely irritating. She had to tell herself quickly that it had only been curiosity . . .

Abruptly she found that they were approaching the flat again, and this time slowing down. As Justin pulled to a halt she was fumbling at the seat-belt. It seemed to stick against her clumsy fingers, and a cool impersonal hand moved across to help her. She opened her mouth to say something just as cool, but he was speaking.

'Give my love to Caroline. If, of course, you think that's suitable. What an extraordinarily pretty girl she is, isn't she?'

'Yes,' Vivien said shortly, casting him a look between wariness and accusation. He hadn't denied anything about Dolores.

'I'm glad there's something we can agree on! Good night!'

Vivien got out of the car and crossed the pavement in a confusion of mixed feelings. Then she spent the rest of the evening alone in the flat wondering why she should feel dispirited. Maybe it was just because Justin Baron was as smooth and untrustworthy as she'd once thought him, and it seemed a pity when she had seen him in a different light with Philip . . . But she ought to have known better than to soften towards someone who was too glamorous to be anything but spoilt; and if Caroline couldn't see that Tom was worth two of any glossy young specialist with an air of only having to reach out his hand to get anything he wanted, that was her look-out. All the same, Vivien wasn't going to go around delivering his messages for him, no way!

She arrived at the Harraday Clinic the next morning to find that Philip had early morning visitors. One was his uncle, looking spruce and extremely cheerful. The other was a small, round, grey-haired elderly lady who was talking to Philip in a thick foreign accent. She looked round from the bedside and gave Vivien a beaming smile.

'Ah, this is the little Philip's nurse, yes? He talk so much about you! I am Mrs Ohlman, I look after the flats where 'e stays, I am what the French call concierge. The little Philip is getting better, yes?'

'Oh yes, he looks much better this morning! Good morning, Dr Baron.' Vivien gave her best smile for Philip's benefits as she spoke. Justin was looking at her so deadpan that she could only suppose he was waiting to see if she would offer Philip the reassurance that they were now the best of friends.

'Good morning, Nurse Challock. Dolores——"

He paused long enough to be aware of Vivien's jump. The small elderly lady looked at him questioningly. 'Dolores,' he went on smoothly, 'if you want to stay a while I'm sure you won't be in Nurse Vivien's way. Or—ah—am I jumping to conclusions?'

'Of—of course Mrs Ohlman won't be in my way,' said Vivien hurriedly.

'That is vair kind, nurse. The early morning is my best time, and Justin could bring me.' The small elderly lady whose name just happened to be Dolores beamed at Vivien again. 'How pretty you are, with your pink cheeks and your blue eyes!' she said amiably, as if Vivien's flush was something quite normal, then turned back to pat Philip's hand. 'And you, my little man, we shall have a chat while the nurse works, and then I must go back to see to all my people in the flats!'

'Mind you take a taxi back, Dolly. The receptionist downstairs can call you one. I must be off.'

Justin came stepping past Vivien where she stood frozen near the door. As he came up to her he paused, his lips twitching, but with a gleam in his eye that reminded her irresistibly of Philip when he was winning some competitive game.

He might have told her last night—but his mocking expression of triumph somehow made her catch her breath on laughter. She swallowed it hastily, and turned it into a smile towards the bed where Philip was thoroughly enjoying Mrs Ohlman's company.

It proved a good distraction against his apprehension about seeing 'a *nuther* doctor' and when the paediatrician Justin had called in to see him arrived at about six o'clock in the evening, he was both pleasant enough and experienced enough to still the small boy's fears. His opinion seemed to be reassuring too, and he said openly in front of Philip (and *to* Philip) that it obviously *was* glandular fever, even if that illness made a habit of being difficult to diagnose. Then he went on to give the small patient a simple description of what the illness was, and what it did, and how it simply needed patience to get it better; all of which made Philip feel both important and more cheerful. There was relief in Justin's face too, quickly masked; and when Vivien went off duty it was with a lightness of heart.

She found a scrawled note from Caroline propped on the dining-table. 'Gone round to see Candy to borrow some gear, might see you later but I'll probably be back late. Had lunch with Justin today!!!' (A large drawing of a heart.) 'Why didn't you tell me it was his nephew you were nursing? Does he look like him? Not that anyone *could*! Love and stuff, Caroline.'

He obviously hadn't wasted any time making sure Vivien didn't queer his pitch with rumours. For some reason that dry thought dimmed her good humour for a moment, and she set to with a cross energy to tidy up the chaos in which Caroline has left the flat.

Over the next few days Justin seemed to be pursuing a positive campaign, to judge from the number of dates they seemed to manage to fit in despite his work schedule. That ought to have made Vivien feel less guilty to find herself the recipient of a letter from Tom—with the envelope typed, which was obviously so that Caroline wouldn't recognise the writing—which began 'Darling Viv' and seemed to assume they were now definitely a pair. With Caroline taking a break from work and therefore there to run into in the flat from time to time, Vivien almost raised the subject—except that Caroline's conversation was all Justin, Justin, Justin.

'I really am in love with him. Oh, did you know his father was something high in the diplomatic service, and was a sir?'

'No, I didn't,' said Vivien 'I vaguely remember Philip said something about both his grandfathers being dead, that's all—but as he seems to take a delight in mentioning that people are both important and dead, I didn't take much notice!'

'I wonder if they're all frightfully Catholic? No, I remember now, Justin isn't, he said something about following his father's religion while his sisters went with their mother, so it must have been a mixed marriage, mustn't it? Shows they can't be utterly against that, doesn't it . . .' Caroline clasped her hands and looked dreamy. 'His mother's out in America at the moment because one of his sisters lives there and she's having a baby. I wonder if he'll invite me to meet her, if she calls in on London on her way back? *That* would be a good sign, wouldn't it!'

'Goodness, is it *that* serious?' Vivien asked lightly.

'Why not? You know, I do rather wish he'd asked me to nurse his nephew instead of you. Still, I suppose it might have been awkward——'

'Because he could hardly treat you like part of the furniture during working hours?'

Vivien tried not to say the words drily—or to recognise that they were scarcely true. Justin *didn't* exactly treat her as part of the furniture; unless of course he made a habit of turning on the charm to chairs and tables as well as people. If she hadn't known, from the occasional mocking gleam in his eye, that he was only treating her to a deliberate friendliness for Philip's sake, she might almost have believed in it. As it was she had taken to treating him with her best nursing tranquillity and smiling at him in exactly the same way she smiled at Philip.

The boy's temperature was still going up and down with monotonous regularity. It was a surprise when Justin raised the subject of his discharge—and there was even more of a surprise in what he said.

'By the way, I didn't mention it, did I? When PJ's stabilised and well enough to be moved I'll want you to escort him home. He's grown so attached to you that you'd certainly be the best person to handle him on a long journey.'

'You mean to—to Malta?' gasped Vivien.

'That's where he lives. Don't look so surprised! He can't stay here indefinitely, so the best idea would be to move him as soon as he shows signs of being really better!' He studied Vivien's wide-eyed stare and asked drily, 'You wouldn't have any objections, would you? Someone whose permission you need to ask before you can fly out of the country, or anything like that?'

'No, of course not!'

'Good, we can consider it fixed, then. Don't mention it to him—I hardly need say that, do I? Offered that sort of prospect too soon, he'll only get worked up enough to send his temperature through the roof!'

He walked away before Vivien could answer him and left her to her sudden feeling of excitement. She supposed he couldn't be free to travel with Philip himself, and it did make sense for the child to have an escort he was used to. Malta, though, and a trip to the Mediterranean—that was really something! Perhaps she'd even be able to stay for a couple of days after delivering Philip to his mother—and see something of the island which had recently been catching at her imagination . . .

She decided she had better not count on it in case Justin suddenly changed his mind, but she checked her passport just the same, and actually found a guide to Malta to buy in a bookshop. She pored over it surreptitiously but with fascination, telling herself that even if she didn't go there, reading about it would help her to keep up with Philip's conversation. There were three islands in the Maltese Archipelago—Malta itself, the smaller Gozo, and the tiny Comino which lay between the other two. Malta itself, though, was the one which really intrigued her—the island of the Knights of St John; the place which had gained the George Cross during the second world war, too, the only time a whole island had ever been awarded a medal for bravery.

It was odd to feel a sharp pang of regret to think that once she had delivered Philip home her job with him would be over. She *had* grown very fond of him. It was only that, and she assured herself of that quickly. It certainly wasn't that she would miss her patient's uncle's daily visits. She would still hear about him, she told herself grimly—and probably see him too if his affair with her flatmate went in the direction Caroline obviously wanted it to. Who knew, she might even end up being a bridesmaid. Unless she'd taken off to live in the Midlands with Tom, which seemed to be his latest, if not quite stated outright, plan.

She put that thought away and concentrated on treating Justin with a formal friendliness and Philip with a placid cheerfulness. Everything else could wait. It was more important to note thankfully that Philip's temperature had stayed down two days running—that he suddenly seemed to be picking up and feeling much better.

Then—even more suddenly—Justin was giving her clipped instructions after summoning her outside Philip's door.

'Can you be ready to leave the day after tomorrow?' he asked. 'I've managed to make reservations for a night flight. Your passport's in order and everything?'

'Yes. You actually do want me to escort Philip home?'

'I said so, didn't I? I trust *you* haven't changed your mind?' There was a sudden frown. 'I hope not, because I've just been on to your agency. I'll want you to stay out there, so I've made it a booking for six weeks. Satisfactory? You'll get usual nursing rates, and your fare both ways, of course.'

Vivien gulped. His casual assumption that she could be free to travel abroad for six weeks at the drop of a hat was shattering, but she didn't care. 'Quite satisfactory,' she said, swallowing on excitement and trying to look completely calm, and as if she had expected it. 'What—what time did you say we're flying?'

'Midnight. You can have some time off during today and tomorrow to sort out your clothes and do your packing—but don't say a word about it to PJ. I'm not telling him until just before we leave for the airport. I'll tell him the truth when it's time for us to set off; then I'll bring him to collect you on our way.'

He would be seeing them on to the plane, Vivien supposed. 'I'd better work a normal day shift on the day we're travelling so that he won't know anything's different,' she said quickly.

'Yes, that sounds sensible. By the way, it'll be hot in Malta during the day but cool at nights at this time of year, so pack accordingly. My sister won't expect you to wear uniform, so you needn't bring that. Now— unless there's anything else you want to ask—I've got to go and make some arrangements of my own. But I'll repeat—go back in there, and *don't* show PJ that anything's up!'

Vivien gave him an involuntary grin. 'I won't. Thank you, Dr Baron!'

She drew a breath, and walked back into her young patient's room feeling unreal, but wearing her calmest face.

CHAPTER FIVE

'WHAT exactly *is* this job?' Tom's voice down the telephone line sounded dubious and even a little resentful.

'Just going on looking after the small boy I've been nursing while he's convalescent,' Vivien said quickly. 'His home's in Malta. It's only for six weeks. Actually I was only expecting to make the round trip as escort, so I'm rather excited. I'm bound to have some free time, and there's an awful lot to see out there——'

'I was hoping you'd come up to Edinburgh for a weekend and we could talk some more about our plans. Mind you don't get turned into a servant as much as a nurse—some of these foreign jobs can get a bit iffy, I've always heard!'

'I don't think this one will, but I'll remember the warning. I—I'm sorry I only sent you such a short answer to your letter, but I'm a lousy correspondent. I just thought I'd ring you tonight and tell you about this latest change. In fact I'm being picked up at ten because we've got to be at the airport at eleven, so——'

'I'll ring you back to save your phone bill,' he said promptly, and nobly, and did so. He then spent half an expensive six minutes grumbling that he would miss her, but for the second half sounded so determinedly affectionate that Vivien's ears were tingling by the time she put the phone down. He seemed to be extraordinarily wholehearted in his change of affections.

She told herself she was glad about it; it was consoling; it was very good for her ego; and when she was so fond of him she oughtn't to feel she was being rushed. Life only seemed a muddle because she had had to sort everything out and pack so quickly. She had already had to cope with Caroline's fit of envy because Vivien was flying out to the sun and she wasn't, and Caroline had only brightened when Vivien pointed out drily that she wouldn't really want to be *there* when Justin was staying *here*. That had brought on another fit of dreamy descriptions of how wonderful he was, and Vivien had been quite glad when her friend departed for a night duty. In some ways, she thought sourly, it would be a relief to be out of range of a Caroline so thoroughly in love.

Without Philip, and with her own absence, there would certainly be enough space and time for Justin and Caroline to get as close as they chose. Bully for them!

Vivien concentrated on the journey ahead of her, remembering with awe that Justin had said casually he had 'booked the whole first class so there'd be plenty of room for Philip to sleep'. Such was wealth, and she supposed if he hadn't been able to do that he'd simply have booked a private plane! It was another world from her previous experience of package holidays. She hoped with a touch of doubt that she'd be able to keep Philip calm and stop him racketing about. Someone would meet them the other end, presumably: Justin had yet to give her instructions about that. A thread of excitement caught at her again, though somehow not as strong as it ought to have been—and she distracted herself hastily by wondering whether she would get the chance to see some of the things she'd read about in the guide book —Blue Grottoes, underground temples, historic sites of this and that. And whether she'd *really* remembered everything she'd meant to pack . . .

Then it was too late to think about any of that, because a ring at the doorbell showed the car had arrived. A driver jumped out to load Vivien's luggage and opened the rear door for her. Justin and Philip were visible in the dimness of the back. Philip was in a state of tension which made him look all eyes and angles. Vivien could guess that he only wasn't chattering nineteen to the dozen because Uncle Justin had told him firmly to keep quiet. She climbed in next to him and occupied herself in being the calmly efficient nurse. They had set off before Justin said casually,

'Oh, by the way, I'm travelling with you. Sit still, PJ, I didn't tell you to start jumping about!'

For a second Vivien stiffened, stung by the idea that he didn't trust her to manage. On the other hand, it was a relief that the responsibility would be shared. His remark didn't seem to require any answer, so she simply nodded obediently. Presumably with so many spare seats he had decided he might as well make the round trip . . . Glancing across at him out of the corner of her eye, Vivien couldn't help noticing that he looked just as smooth, and unfairly even more handsome, in the unfamiliar garb of jeans, trainers, and a leather jacket.

Time seemed to pass in a blur. They arrived at Gatwick, as bright and busy as if it wasn't the middle of the night. A wheelchair was produced for Philip, and several ground hostesses seemed to feel that Justin was just the sort of passenger to inspire their best smiles. Vivien bit back the cynicism and they were swept through the formalities. Soon Philip was being carried up a separate ramp into the plane and a stewardess appeared to help them strap themselves in for take-off. Vivien was seized with a dazed feeling of unreality which she tried not to show, and at last the revs of the engine increased until there was a sharp feeling in her stomach and she knew they had left the ground.

She had to occupy herself then in resettling Philip in a tilted-back seat with a blanket tucked round him. He was still being quiet, though with a tension that suggested excitement, and a hand against his cheek told her he wasn't feverish.

'I should try to go to sleep again, mm? That's right. No, thanks——' She smiled a refusal at the hovering helpful stewardess who was offering drinks and newspapers. As the girl flitted off towards Justin with a hopeful air Vivien glanced round at the first class cabin, biting back a smile at her own feeling of strangeness. Empty except for themselves, it was luxuriously appointed with widely-spaced seats and patterned blinds at the portholes. Even the carpet on the floor looked pristine. This really was travelling in style!

Justin had kept out of her way while she was settling Philip, and was sitting across the cabin now frowning over some papers he had pulled out of his briefcase. It looked as if he was going to spend the flight catching up on whatever work it was he was studying. Vivien glanced across at him wistfully and supposed it wasn't any use to expect him to talk to her when he was obviously so busy. At that moment, however, he turned his head, met her eyes, and raised a beckoning finger. Vivien gave Philip a light pat to show she wasn't going far and moved obediently.

'If he's left to himself he may go back to sleep,' Justin said quietly. 'You seem to have got him nicely calmed down.' He was studying her with an odd intentness, and Vivien realised abruptly that this must be the first time he had seen her out of uniform. There wouldn't be much difference since she had dressed for efficiency rather than smartness in a blue cotton skirt, matching blouse and jacket, and her hair was up in its usual coil—but his gaze seemed remarkably comprehensive and even quite approving.

'Sit down here next to me.' Justin removed his briefcase neatly and patted the seat beside him. 'I can't sleep on planes, can you?' He sounded just as if he imagined she spent her whole life travelling the world. Obviously he did and took it for granted. 'It's not long enough to do more than drop off, anyway—we'll be there in three hours. You'll have to put your watch an hour forward—Malta's two hours on from GMT. I must also remember to give you some Maltese lire, mustn't I? Still, that will do tomorrow.'

'Thank you,' said Vivien meekly. She had actually looked up the exchange rate and wondered whether she would need any of the foreign currency immediately, but with him here she needn't worry about the arrival arrangements. She bent her head to alter her watch, and tried to feel less aware of a long-fingered hand with neatly clipped fingernails coming into her line of vision as Justin adjusted his own timepiece. His was one of those wafer-thin ones with a smoky face and was plainly gold. There was a light dusting of dark hairs on the back of his wrist, and she found herself staring at their silkiness mesmerically.

'We should get there around four, Malta time. Mona's sending a car to meet us. I hope she won't come herself, but I expect she will.' The voice speaking above Vivien's head sounded resigned. 'Between us we'll have to try to stop her panicking, won't we? She was bad enough when I phoned her, however reassuring I tried to be, with the news that PJ was convalescent now and on his way home!'

'I suppose——'

'What?' he enquired into her pause.

'Nothing really. I suppose any mother would be worried to hear her child had been ill away from her, that's all. Not that I'm sure you're not right about——'

'Nice change to find I'm right about something,' said Justin unfairly, but sounding remarkably cheerful about it. When Vivien looked at him he was smiling at her, and it was suddenly difficult to drag her wide-eyed gaze away from the green ones which seemed determined to study her. She glanced round the cabin for somewhere else to look, and leaned forward to take a quick peer at Philip, but he was lying still and she could see his lashes were beginning to droop.

'I think he's settling, so relax. We've got three hours

of each other's company,' said Justin, stretching a little, '—and then, of course, several weeks. Though *then* I'll just be a stray living under the same roof. I'm not even PJ's doctor when he's at home. You'll have no excuse for that "Yes Dr Baron, No Dr Baron" routine you've been giving me, and we can——What are you looking so riveted about?'

'Several *weeks*?' she asked. 'I thought—I thought you were just doing the round trip, and going straight back to England!'

'No, was that what you understood? I've gathered all the information I wanted for my research, and since the next job is to collate it and write it up, I might as well do that in the sunshine. I was beginning to feel an English winter goes on far too long,' he added with a grimace, ignoring the fact that the late spring had quite definitely been starting and replacing cold rain and slush with fitful sunshine and the green glimmer of buds in the parks. 'I've obviously got spoiled by hot countries, haven't I? You know, I wish you wouldn't look as if I'd thrown a bombshell in your lap!'

'It was just that I thought . . .' Vivien was trying to take in this new idea. A sudden memory made her stomach give a jerk and she was staring at him with abrupt accusation. 'You haven't told Caroline you were leaving London!'

'You really are remarkably protective about Caroline! I can't think why. I should have thought she was well able to take care of herself!'

There was the sudden gleam of cynicism in his eyes. He was apparently walking out on Caroline without even the courtesy of a goodbye after paying her enough attention to give anyone ideas, and he didn't even look faintly guilty about it. Vivien's pulse gave an angry throb which seemed to tune with the beat of the plane's engine, and she opened her mouth to say something, but he was speaking again, negligently.

'I'll send her a postcard to say I won't be back for a while if you really think I should. There, have we finished with that subject? Oh no, not quite. I remembered the other day where I saw that blond giant of yours before. Would you care to guess?'

'No . . .'

'Caroline dropped a photograph of him out of her bag the first time she came out with me. I knew I recognised him from somewhere! She said, at the time, that it was "her best friend's boyfriend" and the picture must have got left in her bag after she'd lent it. I thought she was lying, of course. Though *your* relationship with him did make it look as if I might have been misjudging her. However——'

'You must, mustn't you?' Vivien interrupted. Caroline with her passion for photographs and her easy lies. . . . All the same, she wasn't going to let Justin get away with a callous cynicism if it was all based on something as stupid as that. Caroline was her friend and she owed her that much. 'Tom Ainslie and I are—we're very fond of each other——'

'You and Caroline are sharing him? I'm out of touch with London customs after living abroad for so long: is there a fashion nowadays for men to be communal property?'

For a second Vivien was tempted to claim to be an ardent feminist and to consider all men to be nothing but sex objects. It was an argument which could only cause more complications than ever, so she dropped it, with regret. 'You sound to me as if you're just jealous—unnecessarily, as it happens,' she said coolly, but couldn't resist adding on an acid note, 'If you always go round assuming people are lying instead of just asking them, you've—you've only got yourself to blame for a warped view of the world!'

It was difficult not to cross her fingers surreptitiously considering that Caroline *had* been lying to him—

stupidly, when she could just have said Tom was a former boyfriend. The whole muddle suddenly exasperated her. Probably she ought to write to Caroline and tell her . . . but she didn't really want anything to do with any of it. She gave Justin a cold look, only to find he was studying her, and he came out with,

'Yes, you're quite right, let's forget the whole thing. After all, you and I are here and the rest of the cast of characters is somewhere else. That charge of jealousy, by the way: if you meant that for Caroline, no. She comes into the category of "strictly for amusement". Whereas you, now——'

'*Me* is scarcely to the point,' Vivien gritted between her teeth and trying to ignore the way his eyes were lingering over her and doing peculiar things to her pulse-rate. A strange melting feeling seemed to attack her stomach, but the only thought in her head was that she wasn't going to act as consolation for Caroline's latest man as well as for her last one. She got rapidly to her feet. 'I *thought* I was coming to Malta as a nurse. If you had other ideas, then perhaps you'll find another nurse for Philip once we get there!'

'No, I shan't, and you're not the type to walk out on a job either. Do sit down again, or you'll wake him up when he's just dropped off!'

'That will be your fault, not mine!' Vivien cast a quick glance at Philip nevertheless, was relieved to see his eyes were shut, and kept her voice low. 'I just want to get it established, Dr Baron——'

'Justin. I told you to stop throwing that formal nonsense at me. Sit down, Vivien, and stop glaring at me—and I might even promise to behave!'

His smile was his most charming. Vivien decided she couldn't stand men who could turn on charm with a switch. Particularly not men who were conceited, smug, and made no bones about a love 'em and leave 'em attitude towards women. After all, he had given

Caroline plenty of encouragement to fall so desperately in love with him. She gave him a dignified stare and turned her back on him to stalk across to her original seat beside Philip. The steady throb of the plane's engine seemed to echo the rapid beat of her heart—and she tried to ignore the fact that it was a remarkably sore heart too, and given to brooding over the unfairness of repeatedly playing second-best.

She cast Justin a glance under her lashes, only to see that he had calmly gone back to a study of his papers. That was somehow even worse. How dared he be ignoring her when she wanted to ignore him?

Luckily the stewardess came back in just then, and this time Vivien asked for a cup of coffee and intimated that she would like to read one of the newspapers on offer after all. It would be a distraction against her thoughts, at least.

For the rest of the flight she sat on the opposite side of the cabin from Justin, reading *The Times* until her eyes ached and occasionally keeping a check on Philip, who remained in a deep childhood sleep. Justin went on working placidly through his papers. It suddenly seemed as if the conversation between them hadn't happened at all but was all part of her fevered imagination.

The note of the engine changed at last, the warning lights flashed on, and they were preparing for landing. Vivien had to wake Philip up to strap him in and then soothe him when he was half fretful, half excited. She raised the porthole blind to see lights patterning below with a sharp blank at the edge which must be sea. Malta was such a small island that she almost fancied they must be able to see the whole of it from here, but the patches of light below were growing closer and filling the horizon as the plane tilted and sank steadily. Justin had glanced across, seen that Vivien was dealing with Philip capably, given her a pleasant and approving smile, and left her to it. It was almost impossible again to think that he was the same man who had sounded so cynical, and so odious, and so much as if he was thinking of Vivien as his next passing amusement . . .

There was the lightest bump as the wheels touched ground. They taxied levelly, drew to a halt. The stewardess unstrapped herself, came to see that Vivien had everything she wanted, then took up her position by the door. They had arrived.

Coming out into the air Vivien could sense a dryness behind a cool, sharp breeze. Justin had lifted Philip into his arms, and she trailed along behind them with weariness suddenly catching at her. Luqa airport seemed small and domestic in the darkness, nothing like the bright busyness of Gatwich hundreds of miles behind them. The terminal building when they reached it looked small too, rather scruffy, and remarkably dimly lit. There was, however, a large notice in a prominent position saying proudly, 'Welcome to Malta, the George Cross Island!'

Philip wriggled out of his uncle's arms, insisting that he could walk, and suddenly their small party was surrounded by beaming officials in a flood of incomprehensible language which was obviously recognition and welcome. It was almost like being homecoming royalty, Vivien thought in a daze as they were swept through the formalities with respect, and in Philip's case with an obvious affection.

Vivien was caught by an irrational wish that *she* was clinging on to Justin's hand instead of Philip: it would have been a reassurance amongst the strangeness. Then as they were passed through from one beaming uniformed official to another there was a sudden cry and a voice calling out in English.

'Oh, Pip, my little Pip!'

A girl with a mop of dark curls and brown eyes looking huge in her pale face came hurrying towards them with her arms held out. Philip broke into a stumbling run as his uncle let him go. The girl swept him into a tight embrace and started to cry. Philip promptly started to cry too. The surrounding officials clucked sympathetically. Justin's voice beside Vivien said lugubriously,

'Dramatics. Didn't I tell you?'

He steered Vivien towards the embracing couple with a light hand under her elbow. As they approached she felt him let out a sigh, then he was saying firmly,

'Mona, do pull yourself together, there's a good girl. Where's the car?'

'Oh, Jus, thank you for bringing him home! You should have told me the minute he was ill! I should have been with him! I'll never forgive myself——'

'It's too early in the morning for histrionics,' Justin said dampingly, but he put an arm round his sister and gave her an affectionate kiss on the cheek. 'Let's go home, for goodness' sake! PJ, calm down. Mona, this is Vivien, the nurse I told you about. She's very good for PJ, and I should think she won't be half bad for you either. Oh good, they've found the luggage for us. Now, do you think we could go?'

Mona Mantagna had reached out to wring Vivien's hand gratefully without letting go of her son, then they were all climbing into a large black car with a uniformed driver. Vivien couldn't help noticing that Justin was, unfairly, much better-looking than his sister. Mona didn't have his striking green eyes, for one thing, and her face had an indefinite roundness where his was well modelled. She was plump altogether, though in quite an attractive way, and small, an inch or so shorter than Vivien's own five feet four. She looked very young to be the mother of a ten-year-old.

Vivien's head was beginning to buzz with tiredness and she was barely conscious of a flat road, pale buildings flashing by with a glimpse of arched Moorish architecture, then a roundabout with a massive statue in the middle of it. They passed through a huge gateway and reached steep streets with houses closing in round about. When the car stopped she climbed out of it almost in a dream, and found herself being ushered in through an elegantly high doorway.

It led into a marble-floored hall with doors leading off it and a staircase leading upwards with a fretworked banister. A maid was in attendance, in full uniform at this time in the morning. Vivien, swaying on her feet, took in this much with an increasing blurriness. She was beginning to feel as if she was sleepwalking. Then she heard Justin speaking in a practical tone.

'Tell me where Vivien's to sleep, because it's about time she did just that! She was on duty all day yesterday and then looking after Philip on the flight. The blue room? All right. I'll be down in a minute. Give that child a drink of milk since he's so wide awake, and don't fuss!'

'I'm all right,' Vivien managed as she felt his hand on her arm. 'Please don't bother about me——'

'You're out on your feet. Come along. D'you want anything to eat or drink, or will you be asleep before you could swallow?'

Justin led her up the stairs, opened a door for her, showed her the adjacent bathroom. It was confusing to find him so thoughtful. He gave her a push towards the bed, turned down invitingly.

'You're to sleep as long as you like—doctor's orders. No, don't argue, there are plenty of people to look after PJ for the moment. You'll have quite enough to do once you're back to normal instead of flaked out. I don't think I mentioned, did I, my sister's extraordinarily helpless and doesn't go in for looking after herself. Though I always think she could if she wanted to. Good night, or rather good morning, and sleep well!'

He reached out and touched her cheek with his finger, a light stroking movement, almost as if she was a child like Philip. Then he was gone, the door closing behind him.

Vivien gazed muzzily round the room, trying to grasp that she was actually here. In Malta. In Justin's sister's house, in Valletta, the capital. That walled city built by Grand Master La Vallette for his Knights in fifteen hundred and something . . . Bits of the guide book seemed to weave themselves around her, and it all seemed completely unreal.

What was more, she was here in Justin Baron's company for weeks at a time instead of leaving him behind in London. For a moment her mouth was curving in an involuntary smile. Then, against her tiredness, she tried to pull herself together and remember that he was dangerous—to anyone's peace of mind—and there was a cold cynical side to him as well as his odd fits of kindness, and affection, and. . . . and . . .

It became the most important thing in the world to find the energy to get her night things out of her case; and Vivien was asleep almost before her head touched the pillow.

CHAPTER SIX

SHE WOKE to a feeling of happiness and to bright sunlight glinting through the slats of closed shutters. For a moment she couldn't think where she was, then memory flooded back and she sat up in bed abruptly and guiltily. Whatever time was it?

Her watch said six o'clock, but when she shook it disbelievingly she found it had stopped. She jumped out of bed and made for the window, a tall casement with delicate floral curtains to each side of it patterned in soft blue. There were dark blue rugs here and there on the wooden floor too. It was a pleasant room, if with rather heavy-looking furniture, and felt spacious under its high ceiling. There seemed to be a particular flavour in the air—dust, heat, a general foreignness. Excitement began to tug at her again as she lifted a catch to pull the windows wide, then give a tentative push at the shutters which sent them smoothly outwards.

She was looking out into a wide and dazzlingly sunlit street. It was empty and quiet and there were elegant, tall, yellowy-stone houses opposite with grey shutters as closed as hers had been. She leaned out to peer and felt at once a glowing warmth in the air.

One way the empty street sloped upwards to a corner; the other way it took a gentle gradient downwards and then grew abruptly steeper, long and straight and with houses closing in on both sides. And at the bottom, between golden walls, there was a sudden flash of brilliant sapphire—the sea!

Vivien remembered her guide-book map of Valletta and knew she must be looking at a tiny section of Grand

Harbour. All at once she wanted to laugh with happiness. The Mediterranean practically on her doorstep! A highly historical piece of the Mediterranean too, the scene of dramatic battles from the Middle Ages to the second world war.

She ran to splash herself under the shower in the bathroom and began to dress at speed. There were creases in everything and yesterday's clothes had landed in a heap on the floor, but she picked out the least rumpled of her garments and hung everything else rapidly in a large empty wardrobe decorated with heavy curlicues. A glance at herself in the mirror showed that she looked reasonably presentable for work once she had pinned up her hair, in a yellow cotton Indian skirt and a white blouse. It was odd to think of working at all out of uniform, but she must remember she wasn't here for a holiday. Within moments she was emerging tentatively into a quiet house, and wondering what time it actually was.

The wide shadowy corridor that led to the head of the stairs was a mass of closed doors. She couldn't exactly go round trying them all, so she would have to find someone to tell her which was Philip's room. She set off hesitantly down the stairs, looking round her with curiosity. Everything gleamed with a well-kept and well-polished air and the house was elegantly proportioned, with high ceilings for coolness and the occasional rug rather than carpets on the floors. A chandelier of light curved metal hung above the marble-floored hall whose black-and-white patterning was swept free of the merest shred of dust. It certainly didn't look as if Vivien would find herself expected to do the housework . . .

More closed doors faced her when she reached the hall, daunting her as to which one she should try in search of human company. She drew a deep breath and decided to start on the left. That was a double door with brass handles and looked as if it might well lead into a drawing-room. A moment later she found it didn't, it opened on to fresh air.

She was looking into a courtyard, paved and full of sun and big pots of flowers. In the middle of it, seated at a white ironwork table looking as contented and relaxed as a cat, and quite alone, was a familiar figure. Her movement must have caught his ear, because he turned his head, raised a lazy eyebrow, and smiled.

'Hallo, woken up at last? Come and join me!'

'What time is it?' asked Vivien. 'I'm sorry, I'm afraid I must have slept rather a long time.'

'Don't apologise, I told you to sleep the clock round if you wanted to. Actually it's only three o'clock, the time when most people withdraw for a siesta—apart from the sun-starved like you and me! Do you mind sitting outside, or are you one of those people who suffers from sunburn?'

'Not usually, I go brown quite easily.' The courtyard looked so attractive Vivien felt an immediate longing to bask in it, but duty made her add quickly, 'Hadn't I better go and see if Philip——'

'He's resting, and so's Mona—with him, I think, since she's in no mood to let him out of her sight today. They'll have to get the emotional reunion over before either of them can settle down. As for you, you're definitely off duty today. And about time too. I may not be your official employer any more now we're here—because Mona is—but I certainly shan't let you be bullied into starting work instantly! So do sit down, and stop hovering about as if you'd never learned how to relax!'

His look of pained amusement made Vivien pull out a chair quickly and smile at him. It was a smile with a touch of shyness because he looked so thoroughly as if he belonged here, in slacks and a short-sleeved shirt and with bare feet thrust into sandals, and with the sun pouring down on slightly-curling black hair. It gave him yet another identity. She sat down opposite to him and tried not to feel tempted to stare as if she was seeing him for the first time.

'Would you like a coffee?' he asked.

'Only if it isn't any trouble.' It took an effort of will to sound merely polite about it instead of admitting that he had just read her mind—and she was abruptly aware of being ravenous too.

'From the look of entreaty in your eye, what you need is nourishment. Food as well as drink,' Justin said promptly, proving that she wasn't at all good at hiding her expression. 'Yes? I know, I'll get Tina to make you a *ftira*.'

'Who? And a—a what?'

'Tina's the cook, and a *ftira*'s a type of Maltese sandwich. It's the best snack I know for the hungry. You could have in it, let's see, ham, chicken, fish—all with salad, of course——'

'Anything,' Vivien said quickly, and grinned at him, aware that she must sound as she felt—with her stomach flapping at the very mention of food. 'I was too excited to eat anything last night, so——'

'In that case you'd better have *everything* in it! I shall go and see to it. Sit there and appreciate your surroundings and I'll be back in a minute. It rained for five minutes at dawn, so everything's nice and green!'

Justin walked away with a light tread to let himself into the house. Vivien tried to wake up to the fact that she was here—with Justin being amiably companionable and waiting on her too. Not at all what she had expected out of this job. . . . Her mouth widened into a smile as she contemplated a whole five minutes of rain—five minutes, compared with a wet English spring where it might go on all day! She looked round the sunny courtyard with curiosity, and with a deep appreciative sigh.

Bright flowers in big stone tubs shone vividly all around her and she could swear one plant looked as if it was growing small oranges. Geraniums, this early, cascaded in bright splashes of scarlet and white, and there was a big bush just beside her with shiny green leaves and little orange flowers. The courtyard seemed to be central to the house and on three sides there were windows looking down on it, some shuttered, some not, while the fourth side was lower and had a blank dusty wall. It was from this side that the sun came streaming in and she could see just the top of some greenery beyond the wall as if someone else had a garden there.

Justin was several minutes coming back rather than one, but when he came he was carrying a tray. 'With Tina's compliments, and the staff deserve their siesta, so I waited to bring it myself.'

He put down the tray with its load of coffee pot, cups, milk and sugar. And a plate which looked as if it carried a whole round loaf, sliced crossways and stuffed with goodness knows what and cut into four.

'There you are, that's a *ftira*. Yes, it is all for you, so tuck in!'

He looked as pleased as if he had produced the whole thing by a conjuring trick. Aware that he was watching her, Vivien picked up a segment and took a tentative, mouth-stretching bite. It was delicious if difficult to eat tidily, with layers of crunchy salad interspersed with meat, giant prawns, and something that tasted like spiced-up coleslaw. The bread was rough and crusty and had large air-holes in it.

'Nice, isn't it?' Justin poured out two large bowls of coffee, black for him, milky for her, and pushed hers towards her. 'If anything says home to me, a *ftira* does!'

'Did you grow up here?' asked Vivien.

'No, mainly in England because I was at boarding school there. My father was posted all over the place. Malta's "home" because it was the settled place, with grandparents to visit. We always came here for holidays.' He stretched a little. 'My mother came back to live here when she was widowed, and Mona got married here, of course. How about you—you're from Devon, aren't you?'

She was surprised he should know, and cast him a suddenly wary look. 'Yes. Why?'

'No reason at all,' he said promptly. 'What a difficult girl you are to have a conversation with—what have I said now?' Beneath a deliberately martyred air there was a distinct hint of teasing. 'I also know that you've got several elder brothers and all their names—that your mother used to be a nurse before she became a farmer's wife—that you've never been married yourself and don't intend to be unless you meet the right man—oh yes, and your favourite colour. As you once said to me, PJ's conversation can be very enlightening!'

'How—how very boring for you!'

'Not at all,' he retorted politely, and then, holding up a hand as if in defence while his eyes watched her in amusement, 'All right, all right! We'll talk about Malta. My mother *was* born and brought up here, of course, and is very Maltese. Except that she's a Gozite nowadays.'

'A—what?'

'A resident of Gozo, the other main island, a short ferry-ride away. The Maltese peasant considers the Gozitan peasant superstitious and backward,' he added with a grin, 'Which is an interesting form of insularity, isn't it? And only goes to prove that everyone likes to look down on the nearest foreigner. Malta considers itself urban, you see, while Gozo's mainly agricultural. Though it does have its own walled capital, Rabat—Victoria to you. Then there's the third island, Comino, though that's too small to have anything much. Well . . . the Blue Lagoon which the tourists visit, but apart from that its turning itself into a playground for the ultra-rich, with one highly exclusive hotel and several equally exclusive privately-owned villas. Enough?'

'No, I'd like to know about everything. There does seem to be an awful lot to see for such a small area!'

'Malta has history the way a granary has mice. It also has a rare and highly complex language. By the way, all x's are pronounced sh, and gh's and j's are silent. It looks complicated, but you'll get used to it!'

'It doesn't sound as if I will. I'll just have to hope people speak English——'

'Most do. The English are still remarkably popular for stopping the German occupation in the 1940s. Fortunately, though, no one bears grudges enough to mind German tourists—but a mere forty or fifty years is recent history, here.' His pause made Vivien remember the proud notice at the airport, 'Malta, the George Cross Island.' 'There's so much other history that you'll see a fortress or a dome on every skyline, and certainly every third person will be able to tell you about the Phoenicians, or the Turks, or St Paul! Does history interest you?'

'Yes. At least when it's alive rather than in books. There were all sorts of things which looked intriguing in the guide-book——' Viven broke off and added hastily, 'Though I do know I'm actually here to work!'

'Not all the time. That would be a waste, wouldn't it?'

'Tell me about Maltese food,' said Vivien hastily, taking another bite of her *ftira* and wishing the glint in his eyes didn't suddenly remind her of their conversation last night. 'I—I mean, what else is typical, besides this?'

'You want me to go on educating you? All right, there's *fenek*—that's rabbit—and *timpana*, a kind of pie. All sorts of fish of course, lampuki, dentici, swordfish—' Justin regarded her face with amusement. 'All perfectly edible, I assure you, in fact generally regarded as delicious!'

'I'm sure. It's just that I've never thought of eating swordfish.' Vivien couldn't help grinning back at his teasing look this time—or feeling the pull of his friendliness so strongly that it was like a magnet.

'Oh, you will, and with approval, the way Tina cooks it. I'll tell you what we should do now, if you've finished eating and drinking. Let's go out and I'll show you around Valletta.'

'Hadn't I better go and see if Mrs Mantagna does want me? And how Philip's feeling after the journey——'

'He's fine, and why can't you accept it when I tell you you're not on duty today? Not tomorrow, either. You've totted up enough continuous shifts to bring the union down on my neck if you cared to complain—so here you're going to start with time off. What is it today, Saturday? All right then, your next duty doesn't start until Monday morning, and no arguments!'

It was on the tip of Vivien's tongue to remind him that he had said himself that he wasn't her employer any more. On the other hand, she *did* rate some time off, and there could surely be no harm in letting him show her round Valletta when she would only get lost if she went out on her own. She had only got as far as making those excuses to herself when he was on his feet with sudden energy and moving round behind her to pull out her chair. She was dying to see more of the city anyway, so if he really wanted to take the trouble to show it to her . . .

Valletta looked like a city of dusty gold splashed with dark shadows as they went out into the quiet sunny streets. They strolled past shuttered shops which Justin said casually wouldn't re-open until four o'clock. 'You have to remember the island's long siesta if you're ever going anywhere or want to shop. It'll get hotter than this as we get properly into May, too. You won't always be aware of how hot because of the sea-breeze. Remember that it *is* a hot climate, though, or you'll end up with sunstroke!'

The streets were virtually empty, but a couple of strolling men passed them and smiled and nodded; a priest passed cheerfully on a bicycle with a long black cassock bundled round him; a couple of brown-skinned children played idly on a doorstep. Vivien peered obediently at a palace Justin was pointing out to her, massive and gracious-looking, and remembered that the Maltese people were described in the guidebook as the 'friendliest in the world'. She wondered whether that was true of the *half* Maltese, and glanced at Justin under her lashes. He was looking thoughtful, and abruptly came out with,

'Mona doesn't look too happy. I suppose it's just PJ. While you're looking round as a visitor, you should remember that there's another world just under the surface—church-ruled, highly conventional, keeping itself very private and exclusive behind closed doors. That's the world my mother was born into, and very much the world of Mona's in-laws, the Mantagnas. I have the feeling sometimes that she's letting them smother her. Ah well. Note St John's Co-Cathedral, with typical dome!'

His reversion to sounding like a tourist guide suggested he didn't want Vivien to comment on his remarks about his sister. She looked obediently where he was pointing, and he went on indicating things as their walk took them from broader streets into narrower ones, closing until the tall golden houses almost met overhead. Up above the sky was a clear cerulean blue. Here and there an open archway gave a glimpse into a sun-splashed courtyard. It was beautiful, and fascinating, and caught at Vivien's mind with its sense of past and present linked and mingling.

They were working their way steadily downwards, along streets which had turned into cobbles and broke abruptly into steep flights of steps. Here paint was peeling on doorways, dusty plastic flowers bloomed waxily in windows, brighter plastic hung in strips across shadowy openings to let in the breeze. Two old women in unrelieved black, with seamed walnut faces, sat on wooden upright chairs beside a doorstep and murmured a smiling answer when Justin gave them a polite greeting. Lines of washing strung from top window to top window were blowing dry in the wind. Glancing back up the hill, Vivien saw pale gold roofs and domes and walls all in a jumble, dusty and warm and huddling within the city's retaining wall.

She caught a whiff of sea-smell, but there was no sight of it ahead now. All she could see was a blank wall with what looked like a forest of masts and aerials peeping above it. Then as they turned a corner a steep flight of concrete steps led upwards. Mounting them, they were suddenly on a road which topped the wall, and dancing, shimmering blue was suddenly spread out in front of them below a sheer drop.

Vivien caught her breath. There were boats everywhere—ugly grey tankers, tugs, a barge with a rusty crane, motor-launches. There was even a small sailing boat curving lazily across the far side looking miniaturised and graceful against the working craft. Behind and around as if holding the harbour in its arms the city crowded, a mass of lines and circles, roofs and domes, windows flashing as they caught the sun. And out the other way the horizon widened in a clear spread of vividly blue open sea.

'There you are—Grand Harbour,' said Justin, leaning on the rail which was all which lay between them and the blue Mediterranean below. He lifted his face to the breeze which blew in from the sea. 'This may not necessarily be the prettiest place to view it from, but it's . . . satisfying. Does it look as you expected?'

'I don't know what I *did* expect. It's—it's not hard to see why it was always so difficult to capture——'

'Only just. It's quite hard to imagine it now with bombs raining down all over it, but an awful lot of what's fronting it now must have been rubble!'

'I wasn't thinking of that so much. More of the Turks trying to creep in at night under the cannons of the Knights!'

'And Napoleon's ships moored here?' He glanced at her with a smile. 'You know, you have the excited air of someone who's all prepared to fall in love with the whole island?'

'Why not?' Vivien countered lightly. 'It may be all familiar to you, but it's still fascinating to a stranger.'

'Oh, I'm not entirely immune. Still, I'd better not be tempted to wander around too much looking at my favourite places, or I'll never get any work done!'

'What's your research about?'

Vivien had asked the question with curiosity before she remembered Caroline's saying that he didn't like to talk shop. She expected him to fob her off and go on talking about the harbour. Instead he answered her with a direct practicality.

'The incidence of secondary cancers and their relationship, if any, to lifestyle. Poverty versus wealth, whether there's any tie-up with diet, or climate, or Western-style living. I was working with some fairly primitive people in the Gulf States—Do you want to know about this?'

'Yes!'

'As long as I'm not boring you with my own particular obsessions. All right, then. You get extremes in places like Saudi where the oil income gives everyone a car but not necessarily food. Nomads still living in the desert, high-rise buildings and boutiques in the cities—a study in contrasts. Going out in a Land Rover to run a free clinic for the Bedouin was probably the most interesting part of the job. Why are you looking at me in that surprised way?'

'No reason,' shrugged Vivien.

'You have the air of someone who thought I never touched anything that wasn't a private patient,' he said drily. 'It's possible to be paid very well for doctoring in the Middle East, but that doesn't mean one need do nothing else but live the expensive life!'

'I'm sorry, I didn't mean to look as if——'

'Yes, you did. You believe in jumping to conclusions. We've already established that, haven't we?'

Vivien wished she hadn't made him frown when she had been listening to him with interest as well as surprise. Somehow she *had* seen him as working at the smarter end of private medicine rather than at anything else, in spite of his temporary attachment in the leukaemia unit. As she opened her mouth defensively he went on with a mocking curve to his mouth, 'One should always tidy people away into categories, no doubt. Still, let's stop being so serious and regard the harbour instead.'

Vivien glanced downwards obediently with a pang of regret for his change of mood. Then she caught her breath on a gasp and reached out unthinkingly to clutch at Justin's arm.

'Oh, what's *that*?' she exclaimed.

Small, bright-coloured, with a tall prow at one end, a tiny boat was being manipulated along in the water by a man standing at one end waggling a long oar. It looked extraordinarily dramatic against the modernity of the working boats with the man outlined against the water, the vivid stripes painted round the graceful small craft. For a moment Vivien could almost imagine that it was something out of ancient times come to haunt the present day.

'What are you looking at? Oh, the *dghasa*.' It couldn't be a ghost ship since Justin could apparently see it too. 'It's a ferryboat,' he said calmly. 'You'll see them taking people across the harbour all the time.'

'Are they always painted like that? In all those colours?'

'Yes, it's traditional. Maltese boats have always been

painted, so they go on doing it. It's a legacy from Phoenician days. The *luzzu* are painted like that too —the fishing boats. You'll see whole fleets of them at Mgarr or Marsaxlokk. They have the Eye of Osiris painted on the front too, one each side of the prow.'

'Really? You're not teasing me?'

'No, really. There, it's gone out of sight now. Probably going to pick someone up with a basket of shopping —very practical!'

The little ferryboat with its standing-up oarsman had vanished into an inlet. Vivien stared down at the place where it had gone. Then suddenly she was aware of something plucking at her hair. As she jerked round, startled and ducking instinctively with the knowledge of seagulls swooping and mewing overhead, she caught the wide flash of Justin's smile. The tidy coil of her hair was slipping loose round her shoulders.

'That's better.' He held up a hand with several of her hair-grips between his fingers. 'Time you stopped looking so official on your day off,' he remarked, and plucked another grip which was stopping the dark mane from falling lose entirely. As it cascaded round her shoulders the fresh breeze off the sea blew it around her. 'I have a feeling this is much more the real you. Wild hair to go with a wild temper!'

'I often do wear it loose,' Vivien retorted, deciding to ignore the challenge in his voice and in his eyes. She held out her hand for her errant grips, but instead of his giving them to her, she found her fingers caught and held.

'You really can't get away with all that primness you've been so determinedly giving me when you look like . . . No, not quite a witch, more like one of those ships' figureheads they used to carve to remind poor lonely mariners of what they were missing! Though then, of course, you'd be wearing less . . .'

The way his eyes lingered over her on the last words brought the colour up into Vivien's cheeks, and she tried to pull her hand away. Justin was wearing his dangerous smile, with that look of lazy self-assurance which assumed that any woman would instantly crumble at his touch. 'I am *not* prim,' she retorted acidly. 'I've merely been working for you, and——'

'—making it quite clear that any doctor *you* work for shouldn't step over the line——'

'I can't imagine why you should want to. At least, until we got here, where you seem to have decided that I'm a suitable candidate for your passing entertainment. And as I'm not, would you please stop spoiling a pleasant afternoon?'

Instead of answering he pulled her abruptly into his arms. His face blotted out the sky and as his lips captured hers Vivien's knees seemed to turn to jelly. His mouth caressed hers with a surprising gentleness until her lips parted in involuntary response and her arms stole up round his neck. She was aware of the hardness of his body against hers and an explosion of warmth and sweetness rocking through her. For a moment—a long moment—she was lost in the pleasure of it . . .

A keening seagull cried mockingly overhead and she was suddenly free. 'There,' said Justin caressingly, 'that makes it a much pleasanter afternoon—don't you think?'

Vivien gulped. She hastily removed her arms from around his neck and would have stepped back if the railing hadn't been directly behind her. He was looking so pleased with himself that she felt a strong urge to kick him on the shins. Instead she said breathlessly, but with heavy dignity,

'I don't know what you're trying to prove——'

'Don't you? Then perhaps——'

His meaningful movement brought her ducking out of his arms before he could repeat the experience. 'I think we should be walking back now, don't you?' she said very firmly, and began to move along the harbour wall.

'I'm sure I've seen enough of Valletta for this afternoon!'

'If you say so.'

His amused calm as he fell into step beside her made Vivien long to snap at him that she could find her own way back. Unfortunately she couldn't; she didn't actually know the way. She bit her lip. Still, what was a kiss after all? It was better to ignore the whole thing, or at least to take it lightly.

It ought to have helped but didn't when Justin began to point out landmarks to her again in a conversational voice. Nor did it help that she was searingly aware, as if she could still feel it, of the warm imprint of his mouth on hers. He might be conceited, spoilt, and much too sure of himself, but the maddening acknowledgement seemed to tingle along her nerves that he combined all that with a powerful physical attraction which could draw anyone like a magnet.

As it had drawn Caroline, Vivien reminded herself in hasty warning. And goodness knows how many other females too!

She caught sight of a sudden profusion of wicker cages hanging high up outside a window on a house wall, each of them containing a small singing bird. Earlier this afternoon she would have exclaimed, asked Justin about them. Now she simply walked on, seeking for something casual and impersonal to say. She found it in a bright, 'I wonder if the shops will be open yet? I really ought to buy a postcard to send to my parents.'

'And one for your blond giant? I'm sure you oughtn't to leave him out! Oh yes, look, they're just raising the shutters on that shop over there. I haven't given you any Maltese lire yet, have I? Don't worry, I'll get your cards for you.' He steered her towards the shop, then said in much the same casually conversational tone, 'Of course one might wonder why your tall friend signs his photograph on the back, "To Darling C, with all my love,

Tom.' I think Caroline didn't quite realise I'd seen that . . .'

A sideways glance had taken in Vivien's sudden start and his lips curved mockingly. Then he was turning away to study the postcards, picking out a handful, going into the shop to pay for them. She was left to curse her own confusion—and to wonder suddenly whether Justin's treatment of Caroline was actually due to an anger with her about her lie over the photograph. And perhaps he didn't like competition? However, even as she thought of that, she was also thinking drily that he wasn't the type to have to bother about it . . .

He came back to hand Vivien two ready-stamped postcards, and she was still too confused to notice that he had even chosen them for her. She decided not to make any explanations; let him think what he liked.

'There you are,' he said cheerfully, 'one of Grand Harbour because you've seen it, and one with a map of the island, so that you can put a cross to show where you're staying. Now, round one more corner and you should recognise where you are. I wonder if we shall find PJ up and playing the invalid in the drawing-room? I hope Mona isn't going to encourage him into a relapse. He needs a proper convalescence, but he doesn't need to be coddled while he lies there looking pale and interesting!'

A rueful lift of his eyebrows invited Vivien to share his unsympathetic fears, but didn't require an answer since they had reached the house and he was letting them in through the tall doorway. Anna, the maid Vivien recognised from last night, appeared from an inner door in her trim uniform, but Justin gave her a smile and a wave of the hand to show she wasn't needed, and indicated to Vivien that she should precede him through a doorway straight ahead of them.

They went into a pretty and well-furnished drawing-room which looked out on to the brightness of the courtyard, though half-closed shutters barred the vividness of the sunlight and made Vivien blink to adjust her eyes to cooler shade. Philip wasn't there, but Mona Mantagna was, in the company of a middle-aged man with greying hair and a soft plump face. Mona jumped up from her position on a chintz-covered settee, and Vivien could almost have sworn there was relief in her eyes.

'Oh, Jus, there you are!' she said, looking distracted.

'Yes. Good afternoon, Charles. Brought some more papers round for Mona to sign?' Justin held out a courteous hand to shake the other man's, though Vivien had the distinct feeling that his civil tone hid dislike. Charles, whoever he was, looked very formal against the casual dress of the young doctor, in a dark business suit with a silky sheen, worn with a grey silk tie kept in place by a diamond pin. A real diamond, from the way it flashed and caught the light. There was another, smaller diamond set in the signet ring that graced the smallest finger of one fleshy hand.

'Oh, and this is Vivien,' said Mona quickly, 'the nurse Justin's brought to look after my poor little Pip. I'm sorry, Vivien, I can't remember your other name . . . This is Charles Mantagna, my late husband's cousin.'

Vivien received a limp handshake in her turn from a rather soft hand, though if she hadn't held out her own she thought she might have been granted no more than a nod. Charles Mantagna gave her a polite smile that didn't reached his eyes. He said with a touch of reproof in Mona's direction, 'A nurse all the way out from England? Ah, a specialist perhaps in whatever poor little Philip has been suffering from. Otherwise no doubt you would have used a Sister from the Convent, or one of our local nurses.'

'Oh, I always think continuity's the best idea in nursing children, don't you?' Justin answered for his sister. 'For adults as well, for that matter. But I'm merely the medical man around here. How are you, Charles? Have you and Mona completed your business?'

'I was about to leave. Mona, my dear?'

He possessed himself of Mona's hand and raised it to his lips, then he stepped lightly to the door with a nod for Justin. Anna could be seen to appear promptly in the hall to show the visitor out. As the front door closed behind him Mona let out a small sigh and seemed to relax.

'I see Charles still feels entitled to criticise,' Justin said drily. He glanced at his sister. 'I know he's your trustee, but if I were you I'd tell him what I thought of his interference!'

'Oh, I—I can't——'

'Rubbish, of course you can! And does he always come and bother you with business on a Saturday?'

'It was more of a social call. Mamma thinks—I mean——'

'You don't mean to say *that's* who Mamma meant when she was hinting that you'd been a widow for long enough?' Justin's brows drew together in a sudden frown. 'Good God, you're only twenty-eight, and the man must be fifty!'

'He's only two years older than Lewis would have been. And——'

'You don't have to marry another Mantagna—even if you did love the first one,' Justin added hastily as Mona's lower lip quivered. 'PJ doesn't like Charles much, I seem to remember. Oh, is *that* why Mamma wanted him to make a trip to England? To stop him getting in the way? Well, of all the——'

'No, it wasn't only that, she doesn't think I control Pip properly. And neither do you, come to that!' retorted Mona, showing a flash of spirit. 'Think I can control him, I mean. You always say I spoil him rotten!'

Vivien was beginning to feel she shouldn't be here if they were going wage a family quarrel across her. She gathered herself preparatory to moving towards the door, only to find her movement had drawn Justin's attention. He immediately glanced at her and then said trenchantly, with a distinct lack of patience,

'Vivien's nearer your age than Charles is, so I'll leave *her* to talk some sense into you! If you want to get married again I'm sure you can find someone else who's perfectly suitable. Oh, by the way, I've told Vivien she's off duty until Monday, so I'll go up and see how PJ's getting on. If I stay here I'll only loose my temper with you—and besides, the two of you will need to sort out Vivien's hours and working conditions. I suggest you sit down and get to know each other!'

He flung that over his shoulder as he stalked out of the room. Mona was looking crushed rather than resentful at his autocratic manner, and Vivien composed her expression hastily and offered an apologetic smile towards the young woman who was supposed to be her official employer.

It appeared that by Justin's high-handed lights she had been cast not only as a nurse for his nephew—*and an amusement for him*, her mind put in unwarily—but also as a marriage guidance counsellor for his sister. She was only glad to see that Mona Mantagna was eyeing her with an apologetic look of her own, as if she didn't think so.

CHAPTER SEVEN

NEVER having nursed in a private house before, Vivien hadn't been sure what her position would be. Mona, however, had apparently decided she was family rather than staff, and she was to share family meals and treat the house as her own whether she was on or off duty. She would have breakfast with Philip in his room on her duty days, but otherwise it would be brought to her room. They covered all this with Mona looking anxious and slightly helpless, and she insisted that Vivien must have at least a full day off each week. Also, if she wanted any washing done she must give it to Anna, and she mustn't feel she had to help with anything besides Philip.

It was strange to wake on the first Sunday morning, to remember the previous night and being treated like a guest, and to know that the whole day stretched in front of her in freedom. Vivien jumped out of bed to push the windows wide, smelling dust, flowers, and the tang of the sea carried on a warm wind. A thread of excitement ran along her nerves and she drew a deep contented breath. This really was the perfect place to come and nurse one not-very-sick small boy. At least it would be if . . . She thrust the thought of Justin away and decided abruptly that if she was free she would go out and stay out. That would make it clear that neither of them need entertain each other.

Someone passed along the street below whistling cheerfully, and Vivien drew back quickly in her flimsy nightdress and began to plan her day. Mona had given her an advance on her pay in the Maltese lire and cents, so that was all right. She was already half dressed by the

Open your heart to love with 4 Best Seller Romances FREE

Can you resist the promise of wild, passionate romance...the shy glances, the stolen kisses, the laughter – and the tears? If, deep within your heart, you're a true romantic, then these are love stories for you. Stories that comprise a unique library of books from Mills & Boon – we call them Best Seller Romances. From the very first page you'll understand why these books have enthralled thousands of readers and now rank among our Best Sellers.

As your special introduction to our most popular library, we'll send you 4 Best Sellers, an exclusive Digital Quartz Clock and a surprise mystery gift absolutely FREE when you complete and return this card.

Now, if you decide to become a subscriber, you can receive four Best Seller Romances delivered directly to your door, every two months. If this sounds tempting, read on; because you'll also enjoy a whole range of special benefits that are exclusive to Mills & Boon. For example, a free bi-monthly newsletter packed with recipes, competitions, exclusive book offers and much more – plus extra bargain offers and big cash savings.

Remember, there's absolutely no obligation or commitment – you can cancel your subscription at any time. So don't delay any longer...complete, detach and post this card today. The romance of your dreams is beckoning – don't keep it waiting!

PLUS A QUARTZ CLOCK and a Mystery Gift *FREE*

time a tap on her door heralded Anna with her breakfast tray.

The maid was small and dark and smiling and didn't seem to feel any resentment at waiting on an extra person. She had brought coffee and some very English toast and marmalade and seemed shyly prepared to stop and chat.

'I am to look after Philip while Madami goes to Mass,' she confided. 'He is so pale, the poor little one!'

'He's much better than he was. Thank you for the breakfast, Anna. If Mrs Mantagna's going out to church I wonder if I ought to——'

'No, Miss is to be free all day, Dr Justin said so. He will borrow the car and take you out perhaps, to show you our island?'

'I'm sure he'll be much too busy, and I'm here as a nurse, not a visitor,' Vivien said quickly, wondering warily why the maid should assume her employer's brother would spend his time with her. There didn't *seem* to be anything but goodwill in the maid's innocent brown eyes. 'I've just been working for—for Dr Justin in London. If Mrs Mantagna really doesn't need me, I'll go out for the whole day and explore. Perhaps you'd tell her that I'll be out for lunch, and won't be back until this evening.'

Anna gave a little bob in acknowledgement, and then went on obligingly to tell her that there was a Sunday market just outside Valletta's city walls, which Miss might like to visit. The bus terminus was near there too in case she wanted to go further afield, and buses were cheap and went everywhere. By the time Anna left Vivien felt she had all she needed for her day's plans. She ate her breakfast quickly, finished dressing in jeans and shirt with a cardigan round her shoulders in case of a breeze, and was soon letting herself softly out of the quiet house.

The market was easy to find, set up in what must once

have been a moat round the city walls on the landward side. Vivien spent a couple of hours wandering amongst the Sunday crowds that thronged the place looking for bargains in fruit and vegetables, cheap toys, ironmongery, and even puppies in a variety of breeds. It was disappointing that there seemed to be nothing on sale which was particularly Maltese, but any market could be fun. Then, leaving the cheerful shoppers, she debated whether to go back into Valletta and do some more exploring there, or catch one of the buses she could see pulling in and out of their large terminus.

On impulse she chose a bus to Sliema, since it had figured so often in Philip's conversation as the home of his favourite football team. It turned out to be not far away, just the other side of the harbour and full of glossy shops ranged along a wide promenade edging the sea. Sliema's waterfront was full of tour boats, expensive-looking yachts, and even a largish freight boat moored a little way offshore; and all the shops were open, Sunday or no Sunday. Vivien strolled around happily looking at everything and catching a holiday spirit that seemed to be in the air. Stretching up from the sea there were narrow streets to climb with yellow stone houses with the same faded elegance as Valletta's, and domed churches squashed in amongst them or dominating a sudden open square.

She was enchanted to catch sight of a little girl dressed all in long white frills and with smartly-dressed proud-looking parents escorting her. Then suddenly there was another, and another—and as Vivien came round a corner they were all emerging from a church where they must have been making their first communion. They fanned out across the pavement like a scattering of white carnations, giggling and posing as cameras clicked in the hands of proud relatives.

Sunday seemed very much a family day, with everyone out and about to wander round in groups or sit at café tables in the sun. Bright clothes set off olive skins and black hair. Here and there older women dressed in unrelieved black with a cross as sole jewellery, lending a soberer note, but the air seemed to be filled with a general cheerfulness.

Her wandering, curious steps took her a long way and at one time she found herself passing an area where flat rocks stretched out into the glittering sea, with bathers lounging on them or jumping in and out of the water. She felt a pang of regret that she hadn't thought to bring her own costume out with her. At last, with a glance at her watch, she caught a conveniently passing bus back to Valletta.

She was feeling sun-soaked and contented as Anna let her back into the house in answer to her ring. Then, as she was crossing the hall, the drawing-room door opened abruptly and her eye was caught by the tableau presented there.

Mona was sitting on the edge of the settee wearing a crushed expression with Philip drooping against her with, Vivien could swear, an almost theatrical air of knowing he was the centre of attention. Grouped around like an inquisition Vivien could see two seated black-clad ladies and a third who, in profile, looked fierce, elderly, and ramrod-stiff in the same black, but with the glint of diamonds in her ears and at her throat.

It must be Justin who had pulled the door open, since he came into view wearing a blank expression which looked like reined-in irritation. He caught sight of Vivien and pulled the door shut behind him quickly, his face relaxing.

'Ah, so you haven't got lost after all? You disappeared very quickly this morning!' His voice was low and his intent look made Vivien aware of her sun-flushed face and windblown appearance. 'No, I shouldn't go in there —it's a Sunday family gathering of the in-laws. In fact I'd strongly advise you to come out again with me for a walk before they discover you're here and demand to give you a formal inspection!'

His air of muted exasperation made Vivien's lips twitch on a smile, but she asked with concern, 'Oh dear, should I have been here? You did say——'

'No, you were far better making your escape. I did wonder where you'd got to, though. I'd planned to suggest you joined me for a swim. We could go and have one now, for that matter——'

'It's kind of you, but I've only just come in, and I'm tired.' She had vowed before she went to sleep last night to avoid any of his friendly overtures, just to make things perfectly clear. He would soon give up playing his games if she saw she wasn't going to play them with him. Unreasonably, the thought gave her a sharp pang of regret and brought her chin up. 'Don't let me stop you going swimming, though!'

'You won't. But don't blame me if the assembled Mantagnas find out you're in the house and insist on having you called down! And I don't think they'd approve of skin-tight jeans either . . . though I must say I do!' Green eyes glinted at her in amusement. 'Now I wonder, which is giving you that wary look the most —me, or the prospect of meeting my sister's mother-in-law? I can promise you, of the two I'm far less dangerous!'

He came past her to run lightly up the stairs, on a soft laugh. Vivien was left with the thought that who was the most dangerous was a moot point—when he only had to throw her a challenging look for her to be aware of a tremor all along her nerves. She was halfway up the stairs when Justin came down them again with swimsuit and towel in hand, and she gave him her calmest smile as he stood aside politely to let her pass him. Then he was on and out, whistling a cheerful tune half under his breath and without looking back.

The in-laws departed without any insistence on meeting Vivien, perhaps without knowing that she was keeping out of their way upstairs. To judge by the gloomy atmosphere they left behind them she was glad not to have met them. Philip had obviously been encouraged into a bout of self-dramatisation, and there was a shrillness in his voice as Anna led him past Vivien's door some time later. Vivien resisted the temptation to go and help with him by reminding herself that the extra attention would only make him worse. She was tempted to go in and say goodnight to him, though, just to remind him that she was here—until she remembered that now he had his mother back he probably wouldn't care either way. It was a sobering thought and one to remind her wryly that she was only his nurse.

She went down to dinner to find Justin turning on the charm and insisting on quizzing her good-humouredly as to how she had spent her day. It was suddenly difficult not to blossom into eager answers, with her longing to share everything she had seen. Besides, Mona was rather quiet and left the conversation to the two of them; and Justin, looking sleekly handsome and healthy after his swim, could be remarkably good company.

As long as she remembered to treat him as only that, it would be all right.

Monday brought a welcome routine, and if Philip started out scratchy and difficult she soon had him in hand. He was allowed up and showed her a large number of expensive toys, many of them rather young for a ten-year-old. After a light lunch she settled him for an afternoon rest and then went back down to the drawing-room to clear up the things he had left scattered there. Mona was sitting staring into space in an abstracted fashion and jumped when Vivien came in. She managed a smile and opened her mouth to say something, but at that moment Justin came wandering in, stretching like a cat.

'I've been working all morning and I need a break. Is PJ resting? Well then, how about coming out for a swim?'

His eyes were on Vivien, but before she could answer Mona had chimed in. 'Oh yes, Vivien, do go—I can look after Pip when he wakes up——'

'It's very kind of you, but I'd rather keep to my proper duty hours. Has your work been going well?' Vivien enquired politely. She had been aware that Justin had shut himself up in a small study off the hall all morning. She had even had to suppress a small reminiscent smile to see Anna carrying a tray loaded with a *ftira* in to him for his lunch.

'Yes, thanks, though there's a lot to do to get everything in order. You're sure I can't tempt you to come out? I'm only going over to the rocks at Sliema—the ones you saw yesterday. Still,' he added amiably, and with his eyes showing an amused acknowledgment of the way yesterday's sun had caught Vivien's nose, 'I suppose you should avoid the hottest part of the day for your first few days. Maybe we should get you a hat. Mona, I suppose it's no use suggesting you come out?'

'Oh no, Jus—you know I don't much like swimming——'

'A waste for someone who lives here all year round! And you're much too pale, too.' He gave his sister a look of kindly concern, but when that merely made her flutter her hands helplessly and look at him with an air of guilt, shrugged and took himself off. Vivien felt an immediate pang of regret, told herself off for it sternly, and settled down to pass Philip's resting time in Mona's uncommunicative company.

It was difficult not to think that Mona did seem rather unhappy. She livened a little when Philip was there, even if she tended to be over-anxious about him, and she seemed to have a natural sweetness which made her unfailingly polite; but Vivien couldn't help feeling over the next few days that the young widow led a very enclosed life. She went out rarely and seemed to do very little. It was sometimes almost as if she was existing in a state of suspended animation, and as if her mind was constantly elsewhere except when someone was actually talking to her. She was also very nervy, and even the visits of Dr Laurens, the pleasant grey-haired family doctor who was now in charge of Philip, didn't seem to reassure her entirely that her son hadn't suffered some dire fate while he was away from her, and that it was somehow all her fault.

Charles Mantagna's visits certainly made her worse rather than better. He called regularly—and when he did Vivien was left in no doubt, in spite of his urbane manner, that he still disapproved of the presence of an English nurse when Mona could have employed somebody local. She was also able to see for herself how much Philip disliked his Mantagna uncle and made a habit of glaring at him.

'Charles was here again today, I see,' said Justin drily at dinner. He cast a sapient eye at his sister's expression and added with some haste, 'All right, I'll change the subject! But I do wish you'd remember that whatever anyone says, you don't have to let the Mantagnas bully you!'

'It's all very well for you. You don't have to live here all the time!' Mona retorted with an unusual flash of spirit.

'Well, you would do it. Marry into one of the narrowest-minded clans on the island at seventeen, I mean——'

'We're embarrassing Vivien,' Mona said defensively, but with a pretty dignity. 'Vivien, you're off duty again tomorrow, aren't you? No, don't worry, I can look after Pip myself! I just wondered whether you'd like the car to take you anywhere?'

'I was thinking of taking a day off myself tomorrow,'

said Justin with a promptness which, to Vivien, sounded suddenly suspicious. 'Why don't I take Vivien with me? I've got to go to——'

'It's very kind of you, but the buses are fine—they go everywhere, and they're awfully cheap compared with London. I've planned a trip to the temples at Tarxien,' Vivien said untruthfully and with a sweet smile. Only last night when he had been drawing Mona out over shared childhood memories, she had reminded him laughingly how boring he had found those particular antiquities. Vivien raised her eyes limpidly to Justin's face. 'Please don't bother about me, I can entertain myself perfectly well.'

'It's only a lot of prehistoric stones. Still, people do seem to like to visit it—even if Jus doesn't, because he has vivid memories of being sick there! What was it you said was the second most boring thing in the tourist guide, Jus? St Paul's Cave, wasn't it?'

Vivien took care not to look at him while she made an immediate mental note to claim to be going there next, and then listened while they lapsed into an exchange of memories of holidays with their grandparents here on the island in younger days, during their father's diplomatic leaves. She couldn't help having a vision of Justin as a child—probably an exceptionally handsome child even then—laughing and teasing his sisters and turning lithe and brown in the hot sun. It was an interesting picture to set against the smooth and accomplished man. She almost jumped when he turned to her with an amiable,

'We're leaving you out. Come on, what do you remember most about childhood summers?'

'Oh . . . helping on the farm. Once I was old enough I used to drive the tractor when they were harvesting.'

'There's no end to your skills, is there? If you've told PJ that, he'll be green with envy!'

'He'd probably only say it was better to drive a boat.

He was full of some idea that you might let him, once he's better.'

Vivien could have cursed herself for tactlessness when she saw Mona's instant look of alarm, and Justin cast his eyes up and said quickly, 'It was just a bribe—that if he'll take his convalescence patiently I *might* hire a boat to go over to Comino.'

'Why—why do you want to go there?' asked Mona.

'To do some board-sailing in the Blue Lagoon before it gets too full up with tourists. It's a good place for it. There's no need to look at me like that,' he added with sudden gentleness, 'I did say board-sailing, not water-skiing, and besides, accidents like Lewis's don't commonly happen!'

The words brought it back to Vivien that Philip's father had died in a water-skiing accident, which must explain the sudden stricken look Mona had given him. She felt as if she ought to apologise for bringing the subject of boats up at all, but Mona had gulped and was saying,

'Oh yes, I know. And that I mustn't over-protect Pip—and I shan't, when he's older! Do you want the television news on, Jus? It's just about time for it.'

Since Vivien couldn't understand the news in Maltese she took the opportunity to say good night and go up to her room. Sense told her that she ought to sit down and write a long affectionate letter to Tom: he had made her promise that she would write, during their telephone conversation. On the other hand . . . Caroline was free now, unless she was determinedly waiting for Justin to return, full of forgiveness for his abrupt ditching of her. So perhaps she ought to write to Caroline with a warning.

Somehow she couldn't quite believe that the Justin she had seen in other circumstances was quite as hard-hearted as his words on the plane suggested. Perhaps he was only annoyed that Caroline had lied to him. Vivien was standing in the middle of it all, so she was getting everyone's attention while they all played off against each other. It was a sour thought, and almost one to spoil her anticipation of her day out tomorrow—if she would let it, instead of deciding abruptly not to think about any of it.

She had thought of going to Mdina, the old capital in the centre of the island, called 'the silent city' because no cars were allowed within its medieval walls. She woke in the morning resolved that that was where she would go, and she could always say airily afterwards that their comments on Tarxien had put her off. She made a point of slipping out of the house early so as not to run into Justin, and hurried through the streets deciding defiantly that she was perfectly capable of enjoying her own company. That was certainly better for her peace of mind than letting herself be magnetised by a certain dangerous smile, the challenging invitation in a pair of green eyes.

CHAPTER EIGHT

THE MDINA bus took a circuitous route so as to pick up as many passengers as possible. By the time they approached their destination Vivien was almost used to the fact that Malta alternated between flatness and vertiginous steep hills full of hairpin bends. She could guess too, humorously, why all the buses seemed to be festooned with holy pictures and votive offerings: it couldn't be easy to negotiate twisting one-in-four slopes carved out of rock with a large heavy vehicle crowded with passengers. Peering with interest out of the windows, she saw the way graceful Moorish architecture alternated with whole areas along the coast crammed with ugly modern blocks of tourist flats. Inland from the glittering sea the countryside was a dry yellow, but flowers still burgeoned everywhere, wild azalea bushes covered in a profusion of blossoms, a sudden riot of scarlet glowing against a wall, glossy-leaved bushes starred with dark orange blooms. There were even tiny lemon-yellow flowers decorating the tips of the giant cacti which grew to the height of small trees beside the road. Dusty fields showed a tidy pattern of huge orange melons growing, and other less identifiable crops. As the bus ground its bone-rattling way up the steep approach to Mdina her head was full of contrasts—between the arid spaciousness of flat fields and the crowded towns of the coast; between the cheerful modernity of chattering people on diesel-powered transport and the mediaeval antiquity of this city sticking up like a finger out of the landscape. With steep cliffs on three sides of it, Mdina looked like a watching eyrie above the island.

Most of the alighting bus passengers turned away to

vanish into the streets of Rabat, the open town that skirted this side of the closed old city. Vivien was about to step on to the stone bridge that led across a dry moat to Mdina's massive gateway, feeling that there really ought to be a knight in full armour guarding it, when a car drew up just behind her with a squeal of brakes.

'Well! Now if you'd waited to see where I was going today . . .' Justin was smiling broadly at her from the car's window. 'We could have travelled together,' he finished amiably before Vivien could catch her breath. 'But you seemed so certain you wanted to see Tarxien.'

'I changed my mind at the last minute——'

'Really?' There might have been a touch of mocking disbelief in his eyes, but Vivien couldn't be sure. 'Well, since we've met up here after all, let's call it fate, shall we? Just wait there while I park the car somewhere.'

He was backing off and neatly turning the car before she could answer him. It was just as well, because her heart had given an odd lurch of sheer pleasure at the sight of him, confusing all her resolutions. She stayed obediently where she was, feeling as if a sudden sparkle had come into the day. Within moments Justin was back on foot.

'Right, that's done. It must have taken me less than half the time it took you to get here. Have you been round via every available town and village?'

'Yes, but I enjoyed it,' Vivien said truthfully. 'Besides, several people took the trouble to talk to me when they guessed I was a visitor. Well, they tried—one old man could only manage a V for Victory sign and the word "Engleesh"!'

'Chatting up a war veteran, were you? I told you memories were long here.' His grin answered her own. 'Come on, let's go into the city and I'll show you where the best view is from the walls. You can see for miles, as you can imagine.'

He fell into step beside her. Vivien glanced at him,

still confused by his sudden appearance. 'What brings *you* to Mdina?' she asked. 'You surely can't have come as a tourist?'

'No. I'll have to leave you for a while, to pay a duty visit to an old friend of my grandfather's, but it won't take me long. I'd suggest you came with me, but he's rather frail and has forgotten most of his English.'

'He lives in Mdina? Somehow I hadn't imagined that people actually lived in it!'

'Oh yes. Did you think it had all been turned into a museum? It's still full of private residences, as well as a school and the other co-cathedral. It's not called "silent" because it's empty. Look, you can see now why cars aren't allowed here. The streets are far too narrow. Some of them are wider, but most have only got room for someone on foot—or for a horse, I suppose!'

They had come in through the gate. An Arab influence could be felt strongly here and high grey walls showed iron-grilled lower windows. Vivien felt a sense of past even stronger than Valletta's as they walked along a twisting street only an arm-span wide. Everywhere seemed very still. 'Malta before the Knights even got here,' remarked Justin, 'and it almost feels as if the old aristocracy might have withdrawn here to sulk, doesn't it? Shutting themselves away from the upstart newcomers! Though actually Don Emiliano, the man I'm going to see, is very proud of the fact that he can trace his ancestry back to the Knights themselves, or rather one of them.'

'Goodness, can he? I thought they were supposed to be celibate?'

'They were, but not everyone's perfect. And they were soldiers as well as priests, remember! History seems to suggest that they had a high old time. Maybe they even left something of their adventuring spirit in the air,' he said on an amused note, and grinned as her eyes jerked to his face in immediate wariness. He paused to give her time to retort, but when she didn't went on practically, 'Now, if we just go across this square you'll find a comparatively straight street which leads you directly to the wall. Don't lean over if you get vertigo, there's several hundred feet of drop. I'll be about three-quarters of an hour, and I'll meet you . . . let's see, where?'

'You really don't have to bother. Wouldn't you rather stay longer with——'

'No, you're giving me the perfect excuse to leave without making him feel he has to invite me to lunch. I'm glad you sounded half-hearted for once about not wanting my company. I've somehow got the impression that you've been avoiding me—or at least avoiding being alone with me. I can't think why!'

'Neither can I, so it must be your imagination,' Vivien responded with an innocence to match his own, refusing to be drawn by the challenge.

'It must, mustn't it? After all, people usually only take evasive action when they're afraid of something, don't you think? I'll meet you at the Café Rosa further along the wall—that should be easy enough for you to find.'

It was unfair of him to turn the conversation into a fencing match and then walk away before she had the chance to have the last word. Vivien gazed after him with what ought to have been annoyance but instead came out much more like amusement. Well, she could deal with *that*—by treating him with a sunny friendliness all day, just to prove that she wasn't afraid of anything, let alone him. He wasn't going to get the better of her that way.

She had bought a straw hat by now to keep the sun off her nose, and tipped it forward to shade her eyes as she came out into brightness on top of the wall. It really was dizzying to look down on the patchwork of fields below and the view stretched to the horizon like a map stretched out below her in the heat. She picked out a large dome with a town huddling round it in one direction, two smaller domes with accompanying houses in another; there were churches dominating everywhere. Then she tagged herself on to the back of a group of tourists being shown the sights, but unfortunately their lecture was in German. Finally she went in search of the Café Rosa.

It was done up with a trellis covered with plastic greenery, which seemed a pity. Vivien was just gazing dubiously at a bunch of plastic grapes when Justin came round the corner.

'Good heavens, what have they done with it? Never mind, the coffee's good—or used to be. Let's go in and grab a table on the top terrace before some coachload of tourists arrives.'

'How was—Don Emiliano?' asked Vivien as they made their way up a flight of stone steps to where white-painted tables were set out beneath more trellis work. This upper terrace was built into the city wall, so at least there was the view, as striking as ever from a slightly different angle.

'Chatty. And pleased to see me, I think. He's a retired Professor of Medicine—quite an eminent one in his own small way, in his day.' Justin caught the eye of a busy-looking waitress to order coffee, and leaned back at his ease, looking round. 'This place really has been turned into a tourist trap, I fear. Though I shouldn't criticise—from the islanders' point of view we need more tourism rather than less! There's very little profitable industry since the British pulled out of the dockyard. That's on Manoel Island and used to service the British fleet. Stop me if I'm boring you.'

'You're not.' Just watching him as he talked wasn't boring. Vivien caught herself up on the unwary thought and tried to tell herself that she was feeling a sizzle of happiness just because it was a nice day. And because she could smell the delicous aroma of good coffee as cups were put down in front of them. 'I like hearing about the places I'm in, or whatever! Can I ask you about Mdina, or would that bore you?'

'Not in the least, if I know the answers,' said Justin obligingly, and without looking as if he suspected she was choosing it as a safe object. And he went on being obliging as she quizzed him as to the old city's history, and then the island's long years of occupation and re-occupation by different 'civilising powers'. He was extremely knowledgeable too, as if history fascinated him as much as it did Vivien.

'Come on, I'm going to walk you round the streets so that you've done a proper tour instead of just talking to you! Then we'll go down into Rabat and look for a snack lunch—unless you want a proper meal?'

'No, thank you, it'd probably send me to sleep.' It ought to have been the moment to ask him politely if he didn't want to get back to Valletta rather than playing tourist guide for her benefit. Vivien ignored the thought on the rapid excuse that she didn't want to be accused of avoiding him again. If he wanted to go he could always say so. She smiled at him sunnily instead, let him walk her round the narrow streets and cobbled squares of Mdina, and allowed him to forbid her to take no more than a glimpse into the gloomy-looking Co-Cathedral.

'It's much like all the others, gilded saints and candles and marble and a general air of holy hush, and if you want to do churches you can do them without me! Now, Rabat——'

'I'm confused about that,' she said. 'I thought you said Rabat was on Gozo, though I couldn't find it on the map.'

'That's the other Rabat which was re-christened Victoria by the British. The locals still stick to the old name. They have trotting races up the main street sometimes—no, horses with light carriages attached, not people! You look as if you thought I meant joggers! We'll find out some time when it's on, and I'll take you to see it.'

Justin had given her arm a light pinch for her look of surprise, laughing at her. His warm fingers seemed to send a tingle running up her skin. Vivien tried not to notice the effect it had on her, or the sudden increase in her awareness of him which, for a second, seemed to make her sway towards him. She made some quick light remark about the difficulty of Maltese place-names altogether, and tried not to feel as if his arm was brushing hers deliberately as they walked on out of the old city and down into the more modern Rabat. It wasn't deliberate, of course; and she certainly didn't feel irrationally disappointed because he had behaved no more than companionably for the past hour.

They lunched. They inspected some ornate cardboard decorations still gracing Rabat's streets after some recent church festival. Vivien enquired with limpid innocence whether she ought not to visit something billed as 'St Paul's Grotto', if that was the cave Justin recommended so highly, and got a prompt answer.

'No, and I'm not going to give you the spiel about how St Paul was shipwrecked here in 60 AD and cast out all the snakes because one bit him, either!'

'You just have,' Vivien pointed out with a grin. 'He does seem to have had a great effect on the place, from the number of things that are named after him!'

'Far too much, and stop being such a glutton for tourist information! Remarkable girl, aren't you ever going to stop? I'll tell you what—I haven't had my swim today, so let's make for the nearest suitable bit of coast.'

'Oh, I didn't bring my swimming things!'

'Mm. Pity. We could go back for them, I suppose . . . if it weren't for the fact that you'll probably change your mind the minute we approach the house! Or of course—' Justin regarded her with a gleam in his eye—'we could look for somewhere safely out of the way and take a chance!'

'I don't think so. I'd gathered the Maltese don't approve of nudity, and I'd rather not end up in jail.' Vivien made the words deliberately light so that he couldn't accuse her again of primness, and tried to ignore the way her pulse was racing at the way his eyes had lingered over her. 'You go off and swim, and I'll—I'll go back to Valletta on the bus.'

'No, and you're probably right, more's the pity,' he said impenitently. 'By the way, have I complimented you on the hat? It makes you look——'

'As if I should have ears sticking out through it?'

'Not at all. More like an Edwardian girl in a garden. Ah, I know where we can go if we can't go swimming. I'll take you to see the San Anton gardens, and you can drift about in a green shade under the trees, as a counter to all this serious culture we've been indulging in.'

It sounded tempting in the hot afternoon, if surprising when Vivien had come to the conclusion that Malta didn't have trees. She had only seen bushes and the occasional lone palm sticking up out of the landscape. The San Anton gardens were round the Presidential palace, apparently, but open to the public. Justin refused to tell her more than that as they went back to where he had parked the car and opened all the windows to let out the heat inside.

The San Anton gardens turned out to be as shadowy as anyone could wish. There were trees of every variety and colour planted between a pattern of paths. They had been brought from all over the world to be a park and a screen for the palace set almost invisibly behind a high wall in one corner, and there were formal ponds here and there, and one area with large cages full of brightly-coloured birds. Vivien saw a giggling crocodile of very small children being taken to see the birds—perhaps on an infant school outing—and there was the occasional stroller and a group of obvious tourists taking photographs. Otherwise the place was quiet and peacefully empty, a cool green refuge from the dusty heat. Flowering bushes drooped appealingly behind park benches offering a convenient rest for the weary, and curling paths curved out of sight from a central straight avenue.

'Pleasant?' queried Justin.

'Lovely! Look at those extraordinary bulbous tree-trunks over there.'

'I think I'd rather not. Sit down and look at that bougainvillea up there instead. See, that one? All that feathery purple?'

Vivien had sunk down on a bench obediently. She raised her face to look up, just as obediently.

She felt the straw hat being gently pushed back from her head, and afterwards a small voice inside her mind whispered *'Sucker!'* Justin's arms came round her firmly, and as she was pulled against him his mouth came down on hers with an all-too-well-remembered sweetness that seemed to run coursing through her body . . .

'Too tempting by half,' his voice murmured as his lips released hers. His breath was fanning her cheek and as her eyes flew open he was looking down at her from such close quarters that he was just a dark blur between her and the trees. 'And such a nice private part of the gardens too—I've always thought it was the ideal place for a quiet siesta. Now don't pull away, just when I've got you where I want you!'

She hadn't thought of pulling away from him: there was a kind of magic inevitability about being in his arms again, and the caressing note in his voice had an effect too strong for her to resist. She tried to fight against it and began,

'What a lot of trouble to go to just for——'

'Monster! And I don't believe that cool little voice—not when I can feel your heart beating against my hand!'

His fingers were cupping her breast through her blouse, sending dangerous spirals of pleasure through her. Vivien opened her mouth to retort—if she could —that there was a natural release of adrenalin when someone gave you a shock. She hadn't got the words out before his mouth came down on hers again, harder this time, crushing the breath out of her and parting her lips with his probing tongue so that it felt as if he was taking possession of her. She was lost and drowning, magnetised by pleasure as if she could melt into him entirely.

A squeaky giggle, somewhere very near at hand, brought her abruptly back to sense and set her hands pushing against Justin's shoulders when a moment ago they had been creeping involuntarily round his neck.

His abrupt release of her almost sent her tumbling backwards on the bench. She turned swiftly, swallowing hard, to see that two small children hand in hand had come round the bend in the path and were walking decorously past them with round-eyed sidelong glances. Almost immediately a whole squad of juvenile twosomes filed into view, with a cowled nun in attendance. The infant school must have finished looking at the birds and was now promenading through the gardens.

Justin's expression was a study. He obviously hadn't planned on being interrupted by an audience after his careful staging, and he was fighting a battle between ruefulness and amusement. He was also looking as lazily dangerous as a cat interrupted in the middle of hunting, and far too attractive for Vivien's pulse-rate. She came swiftly to her feet, feeling they were just reaching a point where she might bite off more than she could chew.

'Weren't they sweet?' she said airily. 'Let's walk on and——'

'No, come back here and stop trying to look as if you didn't like being kissed. I can't think of a better occupation for a sunny afternoon. And neither can you!'

Vivien looked at him and her heart turned over. She knew it was medically impossible, but she could feel it happen, quite distinctly. It was on the tip of her tongue to agree and let herself be drawn back to him. Then, suddenly, it became absolutely imperative to prove that she wasn't going to take anything he did at all seriously. She tilted her chin at him, looked considering, and was surprised to find how light and normal her voice could sound.

'Oh, as to that, I was just finding it interesting to see whether Caroline was right as to how well you kiss! Now that I've tried it twice I think I could agree with her grading . . . on a scale of one to ten, you know!'

CHAPTER NINE

'AH YES, I'd forgotten how much you two run your lives in harness.'

Justin got to his feet in the dappling shadows in an almost lazy movement. He was smiling at her, but it wasn't the friendly smile of a moment ago. 'Well now, how about *you* being able to write and tell *her* how good I am in bed? I'm sure we can manage to slip back into my sister's house without anyone spotting us. I'm sorry I can't suggest a hotel, but when one comes from a rather well-known family——'

'No, thanks!' said Vivien quickly.

'Oh dear, what a flat turn-down! And I'm sure she'd be pleased to know. Somehow there wasn't a chance in London for a demonstration.' Justin's eyes were regarding her with a gleam of cynicism. 'Never mind, if you're really not in the mood. Or is it the wrong time of the month?'

The polite enquiry made Vivien want to choke. She didn't, but tried hastily to frame some lofty answer that wouldn't sound simply defensive. Perhaps that she didn't find his offer interesting enough to be worth the experience—now or at any time. A sharp sqeezing sensation in the pit of her stomach felt infuriatingly like regret: how could she possibly still feel attracted to him when he was looking at her in that dislikeable way? She began to frame a sentence which would convey that she didn't need a reason for turning him down when they were interrupted again, this time by a strolling couple admiring the greenery. Justin took the moment to begin to move back the way they had come.

'This place seems to be attracting more custom than I

remembered. Would you care to admire the outside of the palace? Or shall we be getting back . . . ?'

'I'd like to look at the birds,' Vivien said promptly, though trying for a tone as coolly polite as his own. 'I'm sure they're much more attractive than—than——'

'Than anything else I might have in mind? Don't worry, I *can* take no for an answer. It was just the impulse of the moment—to complete our pleasant day. But I don't go in for unwilling company, so you needn't start locking your bedroom door. Though of course if you change your mind, I don't lock mine.'

He offered that so casually and in such a cynical tone that Vivien was almost betrayed into turning her head to glare at him. A sidelong look from under her lashes showed that he wasn't even looking at her, so the glare would have been wasted. She speeded her steps instead, trying to look as if she was eager to see the caged birds and wondering suddenly whether he would dump her any minute and decide to drive off alone. It would probably be better if he did. The laughing companionship of earlier in the day was thoroughly gone, and she shouldn't have been so stupid as to believe it had been enjoyable for both of them—to be caught by the magic of it——

She wasn't looking where she was going as she stepped past a massive tree-trunk into the straight central avenue. She certainly didn't see the speeding teenager on a bicycle, where no cyclist ought to be from the clearly displayed notice on the park gates. For a moment she was only aware of Justin's arm snatching at her in a strong grip to swing her backwards, and she began a gasp of protest which seemed oddly echoed by a gasp of his own as she landed against him with a thump. Then she realised what was flashing past her in a whirr of wheels, with a young face swinging guiltily towards them for a moment before the boy put his head down and pedalled swiftly on before he could catch a reprimand.

'Idiot! You too—*damn*!'

Justin was putting her away from him so roughly Vivien thought for a cross moment that he didn't have to behave as if she had an infectious disease. Particularly when he had shown every desire to hold on to her not five minutes ago. So much for his sophistication, if he could sulk at a put-down, she began scathingly to herself, with deliberate scorn to conceal a feeling of hurt. Then she realised that he was holding his arm away from his body and why. Scarlet drips of blood were coming from his hand and splashing on the path.

'You're bleeding!' she exclaimed.

'I caught my thumb against the tree. I *would* have to hit a sharp spike from a broken branch! Damn it!'

He was reaching in his pocket for something to staunch the flow. As his free hand came up with a clean handkerchief Vivien reached out to take it from him and to reach for the bleeding hand too, nursing training taking over automatically. 'Here, let me. Let me see how bad the cut is too. If you've gashed it thoroughly we'll have to find a hospital to have it stitched——'

'Don't fuss, it's probably only a graze!'

'What, bleeding like that? For goodness' sake, let me look at it—I am a nurse, remember?'

'And I'm a doctor,' retorted Justin drily, wrapping the handkerchief into a pad and pressing it against the wound with a wince. 'So you can spare me your ministrations and let me decide how to treat a minor wound!'

'Oh, don't be so childish, and stop standing on your dignity!' Vivien snapped, shock suddenly catching her from her narrow escape. She could easily have been lying in the middle of the path with broken bones from a collision at that speed, and she glared at him fiercely. 'Doctors are the worst patients alive, do you know that?'

To her surprise he began to laugh. She thought the amusement in his eyes died a little as he looked at her, but she had ducked her head to inspect the hand he was now obediently holding out to her. 'Yes ma'am, very well ma'am,' he said mockingly, and trying not to wince as she lifted the pad very gently from an oozing gash that ran along the fleshly heel of his thumb. 'I suppose your next move will be to offer to tear your petticoat into strips.'

'I'm not wearing one, and I've often wondered how they could have torn them up tidily anyway. It doesn't look too deep. It'll need cleaning up and bandaging, and we probably ought to——'

'There should be a first-aid kit in the car,' he interrupted her practically, 'though even if there is, you're not going to put my arm in a sling just to satisfy your Nightingale instincts. First because it doesn't need it, and second because I've got to drive. And no, *you* can't—for one thing I hate being driven, and for another you haven't got a Maltese driving licence. You have to pass a special test here to stop you driving off the edge of cliffs. May I have my hand back, please? Thank you! And now let's both look where we're going!'

'I couldn't possibly have seen——'

'I'm not actually blaming you,' he retorted. 'I just hope that brat's been caught by a park-keeper before he does any real damage!'

'It's your right hand—oh dear. Are you sure you'll be able to——'

'Driving would have been worse if it had been my left, with a gearstick to consider,' he pointed out. 'Not that I'm that incapacitated, except that I might have bled all over you every time I changed down.'

Vivien thought he was looking rather white all the same, and as if the pain was greater than he was showing. It was all her fault too. If she hadn't brought Caroline's name up the day wouldn't have turned sour and she wouldn't have been stalking along with her head in the air. She thought of the tendons in the heel of the thumb and wished she knew if he had caught one of them: she hadn't been able to see for the welling blood. It was all very well for him to be stubborn enough to insist on taking it lightly, and that was probably simply because he was annoyed with her. She had meant to annoy him; the trouble was that almost at once she had started wishing she hadn't . . .

They had reached the car and he was feeling left-handed for the keys, saying as he did so,

'If by any chance Mona hasn't got a first-aid kit in her car I suppose we can always resort to primitive methods and wash it in the sea. And you can tear up some other bit of your underwear!'

'You will *not* wash it in the sea! And don't give me that old saw about salt being good for wounds, either—there might be just about anything else in the water too!' For good measure Vivien added fiercely, 'And you won't go swimming until it's healed up either, though I presume you wouldn't be such a nut as to risk getting it infected!'

'Remind me never to be one of your patients, you're extremely bossy,' sighed Justin. 'I've washed in sand before now without suffering from it. The only thing that's annoying me is the thought that I'm right-handed and this is just the moment when I've got a lot of writing to do. Ah, there *is* a box with a red cross on it: let's see what's in it.'

He had sat down to peer into the car's glove compartment, and Vivien couldn't help suspecting that he was actually quite glad to be sitting down for a moment. There was a tightness around his mouth and blood was running down his wrist again in spite of the padded handkerchief. His voice had suddenly held a crosser note too. She took the tin box firmly from him and was glad to see gauze and lint in sterile packets, two small bottles with one of them marked White Spirit, and several rolled-up bandages.

'No butterfly plasters, but I suppose they wouldn't stick with the blood. Never mind, just——'

'If it does need a stitch you'll go to a doctor and have one!' Vivien told him. 'Can you move your thumb to and fro?'

'Yes, I can, I'm only not because I want to stop dripping!' he said irritably. '*Will* you stop giving me orders? All right, just clean it up for the moment and bandage it—oh, and slap some of that iodine on it while you're about it.'

She had as he said, working carefully and gently and hoping she wasn't hurting him too much. It didn't actually look too bad now she could see it properly, and a firm pad of gauze stopped the bleeding. The iodine must have stung, but he hadn't flinched. As she wound a bandage expertly into place and Justin watched her in silence, she couldn't help thinking guiltily that it wouldn't be very easy for him to write for a few days. His bent head as he watched her, and his slight frown, were suddenly sending pangs of acute regret through her for disliking him so much fifteen minutes ago. On the other hand, she did have good reason to take him lightly—as lightly as he undoubtedly took her. 'There,' she said, trying to sound efficient about it, 'that should hold all right. Just don't—don't grab at anything for the moment.'

'No, I've rather been cured of that, haven't I?'

He could have meant anything, even in that lightly sardonic voice. Vivien decided to ignore it. 'I hope it's reasonably comfortable. I quite see that you can't let me drive, but——'

'No, I can't!'

'I was just going to say, I haven't actually thanked you for stopping me crashing into that bicycle. I'm sorry you got hurt doing it. And look, If—if writing's going to be difficult perhaps I can help. You could show me which order you want to put things in and I could copy them up for you in the evenings after Philip's in bed. Or dictate to me, if you did it slowly. Truly, I mean it!'

'I believe you do.' Justin had raised his eyes to her face. For a moment he almost looked as if he would accept her suggestion in the goodwill in which it was offered, then the dawnings of a smile were blanked out. 'I'll bear it in mind, at suitable secretarial rates,' he said coolly, 'though I'll hope not to have to bother you. Now, if you'll just shift over and put your seat-belt on, we may as well go home.'

His expression didn't encourage Vivien to say that she hadn't meant to charge him secretarial rates. His expression didn't actually encourage anything at all, and he had thrown the first-aid box into the back and was clipping himself in efficiently. He drove silently, capably, and as impersonally as if he had a stranger beside him all the way back to Valletta, and Vivien tried to tell herself that she was perfectly happy to have him that way. It was certainly better than being sexually propositioned with a casualness which showed just how much of a passing amusement he considered her. As an 'occupation for a sunny afternoon.'

Instead of ending up in bed they had ended up amongst the bandages. There was a farcical element to that, and it served him right—except that she did hope his hand wouldn't get infected, or turn out more seriously hurt than he was admitting, or give him too much trouble . . .

It didn't appear to, since he took himself out for the evening. He went out all next day too and didn't appear for any meals. Vivien was conscious of missing him. She had grown far too used to his being there across the dining table to chat and smile and exert his lazy charm. Mona was more subdued without him too, sinking back into her tendency to jump at shadows. She had had her head snapped off for flapping because Justin was wearing a bandage—but when Vivien came down from putting Philip to bed on the third day and felt an involuntary lift of the heart because Justin was actually in evidence, she placed herself in front of him with a mixture of meekness and determination.

'Would you like me to re-dress your hand?' she asked.

'No, thank you, I got a friend to do it. You remember Christiane?' Justin enquired, moving over to speak to his sister. 'She's walking the wards as a registrar now.'

'Didn't she marry——'

'No, she broke it off—too much risk of being expected to stay home and have babies instead of pursuing her career. It was fun to look her up again. She sent you her regards, by the way, and was sorry to hear about PJ's glandular fever. We found we had quite a lot to catch up on.'

Vivien felt put in her place, and went on feeling it as he spent the meal discussing mutual friends with Mona. He went out again directly afterwards too. Perhaps to meet the unknown Christiane. Vivien felt a stab of unexpected jealousy and told herself quickly that she wasn't feeling it. She didn't want his attention, so why should she?

Philip had picked up enough to be allowed out for a drive with his mother in the car. That gave Vivien an extra free afternoon, and she took herself over to swim from the rocks at Sliema in the warm and silky water. She felt oddly wistful because Justin might have been with her and wasn't. What on earth was the matter with her these days?

She could plan her next day off instead of catching herself out in brooding over the mixed emotions of the last one, and a certain person's total indifference to her since then.

The ferry trip to Gozo might be appealing if she set her mind to it. Justin obviously wasn't going to repeat his offer to take her over there now. And just as well, when spending too much time with him sent her into a state of disturbance where her skin seemed to prick with restlessness, so that behind a deliberately tranquil face she was growing almost as jumpy as Mona.

She would have gone to Gozo, and had it all planned, if Anna hadn't mentioned that, 'Dr Justin has gone off early to catch the ferry, he has some friends to see on the other island.' Vivien might not run into him, but if she did it might look as if she was following him. She caught the bus to Mosta Dome instead, admired its beautiful interior which was a lot more peaceful than she was feeling, then tried rather drearily to think what to do with the rest of a lonely day. Swimming again, she supposed—and at least that would be enjoyable, and she might as well improve her tan!

She went back to Valletta feeling somehow subdued, only to find that she had forgotten it was Sunday (in spite of a service going on in Mosta Dome) and the Mantagna relatives were paying their formal afternoon visit. Being inspected by what seemed like a large number of formidable Mantagna ladies in the company of the inevitable Charles was really no joy, and she could feel them oozing with disapproval for her shorts and sun-top. Luckily she was dismissed after five minutes, very much as if she was a servant, and could retreat to her room feeling sorry for Mona. No wonder Justin had gone out for the day! The way Mrs Mantagna senior said, 'So this is the nurse your brother brought,' over the top of Vivien's head suggested she didn't think much of her daughter-in-law's brother, either. There was a distinct feeling in the air that no one could be approved of who wasn't totally Maltese, and not given to doing anything so foolish as gadding round the rest of the world.

Philip's improvement since his arrival home was so marked by now that Vivien almost did feel a nurse wasn't necessary for him. She had only done three of her six weeks, but she began to wonder a little dispiritedly whether she would be sent home early. However, Philip still needed a companion since Dr Laurens didn't feel he was ready to start school again yet, and there was certainly plenty to do in keeping him occupied. Visits from his paternal relatives almost always made him revert to seeming thoroughly spoilt, and Vivien couldn't help feeling that her in-laws really didn't make Mona's life any easier, and she coped patiently with Philip the following day.

'Why did Mummy have to go out this afternoon when I *want* her?' the boy asked fretfully.

'I don't know, love, was there some special service she had to go to with the rest of the family? Oh, and while I think of it, wasn't there a letter your grandmother said you must write? Why don't you do it now and get it out of the way?'

'I don't see why I have to. Aunt Isabel only sent me a card, not a present.' It was a gloomy enough card to have sent to a child too, with purple flowers and a long and complicated prayer in it. 'Anyway,' Philip added mutinously, 'I hate writing letters!'

'Yes, but sometimes you have to, to be polite,' Vivien explained. 'I'll tell you a secret, a true one. I hate writing anything, but particularly letters, so I hardly ever do—and not long ago I got into awful trouble for not writing a letter when I should have done. So you see it's just as well to get them out of the way!'

'What was the letter you didn't write?' Philip demanded with his usual need to know everything.

'One signing off from a job. And then everyone thought I hadn't done it on purpose. So you see——'

'Oh, that was how it happened, was it?' Justin's voice said from the doorway, making Vivien jump. She could have sworn he wasn't in the house. The sight of him standing there now made her heart give a sudden lurch and she hoped her jump looked like nothing but surprise. He came further into the room, looking remarkably amiable. 'I'll tell you something, PJ, and you can take a lesson from it. Vivien's just admitted that she hates writing anything, but she still offered to copy up my notes for me.'

'I still will, if——' Vivien began.

'It's all right, I've managed to borrow a typewriter. I've just brought it in. It'll be a two-fingered job, but it'll probably be more legible than my handwriting anyway. You see, PJ, there are ways round everything.'

'Uncle Justin, *when* are you going to take me out in a boat? You promised——'

'I haven't forgotten, but it'll have to wait a while. I can't go board-sailing with a bad hand. Though, like you, it's steadily getting better,' Justin added, ruffling his nephew's hair affectionately. 'I'll tell you what, though, I'll let you try out the typewriter instead. You might even manage whatever this weighty correspondence of yours is! What was Vivien trying to persuade you to do, write a letter to Dolly?'

'No, to Aunt Isabel, because I'm supposed to, because she sent me a *card*—I wouldn't mind writing to Dolores,' Philip added, dropping the sulk quickly in favour of this new idea. 'Can she come out and see us? Can Vivien write to her too? Can I really use the typewriter? Can we do it now?'

'Heavens, what have I started?' Justin enquired of the air, but he seemed good-humouredly inclined to help Vivien out in her amusement of his nephew. Remarkably so. It was as if he had suddenly decided to acknowledge her again as he raised a humorous eyebrow in her direction and then took them both off into the study, where he displayed remarkable patience in helping to discover how to do capital letters and where the commas were.

'Much like a computer keyboard. Maybe I should have got one of those and sorted out my notes via word-processor. I was going to start doing that at the hospital—if I hadn't come out here instead.' The remark seemed to hold some particular meaning, though Vivien chose not to turn round to see what it was, when he was standing so close behind her directing operations that her awareness of him was making her feel breathless. 'They say everyone gets bitten by an obsession at some time in their lives, don't they? However irrational.'

'Will you get me a computer, Uncle Justin? Several of the boys at my school in England had micros at home—I told you——'

'And *I* told *you* I'd think about it before your next birthday. I'm certainly not going to get you one between birthdays,' his uncle told him firmly, and slid an arm round Vivien to detach Philip's fingers from a constant pressure on the repeat space. 'Stop making that sound like a machine-gun, or I shall switch the whole thing off! Yes, better. And that sounds like Mona coming in.'

The abrupt silence as Philip's fingers were removed from the keyboard brought the sound of a slam of the front door and the click of high heels across the hall. A second later the world seemed to shake itself back to normality as she came into the room, and Vivien stopped being caught by sharp memories as Justin moved away from her. It was no use feeling like that, but she did—and as if her body's betrayal might show in her face, making her give an unnaturally bright smile at an abstracted Mona.

Justin stayed in for the evening and was back to his lightly charming self. He was in all next day too, the sporadic tap of the electric typewriter showing that he was working. Philip was allowed out for a short walk in the later afternoon and had to be restrained from jumping about gleefully when he went with Vivien to post his letters. Even that small amount of activity tired him more than he wanted to show and pointed up the reason for Dr Laurens' carefully slow convalescence programme: glandular fever was subject to recurrence, and because Philip had caught it at an unusually young age they were being particularly careful. When they came in again he seemed quite glad to sit down leaning against his mother and watching television quietly. Vivien hesitated, then asked,

'Would it be all right if I took an hour off and went for a swim? I won't if you'd rather I didn't.'

'Yes, do go. Shall I dig Jus out and get him to take you? He's been working all day and I'm sure it's time he stopped.'

'I wouldn't want to disturb him.' It was ridiculous to sound so half-hearted; to have gone from avoiding him to feeling a stab of wistfulness over not having seen him all day. He was probably swimming again by now too: she had noticed last night that he had changed his bandage for a light plaster strapping. 'If—if he comes out before I go I'll ask him, otherwise I'll leave him in peace,' she said quickly, and went to run upstairs for her swimming things, making a deliberate point of doing so audibly.

It was disappointing when she came down again to see the study door still firmly shut. It was just that he had been friendly last night, that was all—not quite his old challenging self, but friendly. Vivien had spent half the night telling herself, though without much conviction, that that was just how she wanted him to be. And that there was no harm in having a thoroughly civil relationship, now that everything else had been established. And that she *didn't* feel extraordinarily weak at the knees every time she remembered their day together in Mdina . . .

She had a quick dip and came back with a sparkling feeling of renewed energy. She was just coming out of her room when Justin came out of his.

'A rather damp mermaid,' he observed, regarding her hair which had gone into a fuzz after a quick towelling. There was a quizzical look in his eyes. 'Why didn't you wait for me, though?'

'I thought you were busy.'

'I wouldn't have minded being dug out.'

For a second he was giving her a look that suggested he was going to accuse her again of avoiding him. Rather than start the whole pattern again Vivien broke quickly into speech with a careful smile.

'You might have been in the middle of something, and I thought I wouldn't be popular if I disturbed your concentration. The water was lovely, so it's a pity you didn't come. At least, as long as your hand's properly healed—if it isn't I wouldn't have let you go in!'

'Bossy—didn't I say so?' He stretched and grinned, then turned his head at the sound of someone moving in the hall below. 'I've just promised PJ I'll play him at Buccaneer before he goes to bed. Come on, you can play too—it'll make a better game with four of us, and I have the feeling that you might make rather a good pirate!'

Mona had already got out the board game for her son and even seemed prepared to join in the competitive atmosphere which immediately seized Justin and Philip. Vivien had the rules explained to her—it was all to do with collecting treasure and fighting sea battles—and they were soon deep into desperate forays across the squares of the board. There was suddenly such a likeness between Justin and his nephew as they both triumphantly shouted 'Attack!' or seized each other's treasure, or robbed nearby ports, that Vivien was hard put to it not to laugh.

She did join in the teasing as Mona pretended a lofty maternal tolerance towards both males.

'Honestly, Vivien, would you think he was my *older* brother? I mean, just look at him lying there on the floor!'

'I think there's a sociological expression for it—"playground regression" or something.' Vivien said it straight-faced and dodged as Justin reached for her wrist in a pretended slap.

'You can stop sounding like an infant school teacher

and concentrate on the fact that my ship's about to come up on you fast. Aha, you thought it was PJ I was aiming for, didn't you? Whereas in fact——'

'You lose, because I shall play my Yellow Fever card and send you into quarantine. See how you like that!' Vivien retorted sweetly, her mouth curling in a triumphant smile.

'Oh, you wretch. Can't I appeal? If you do that, either PJ or Mona will get into port any minute and win!'

'Good. And you didn't say anything about making alliances, so it's no good suggesting one now.'

There was suddenly something mischievous behind the challenge in his eyes and his lips parted as if he would say something. Whatever it was, to cause an undercurrent in the air between them, was lost in Philip's crow of triumph and his, 'It's my move next, so even Mummy can't beat me!' Vivien felt Justin's eyes holding hers and couldn't look away. There was a sudden wealth of meaning in the way his lips twitched and one eyebrow went up.

'Funny, I thought I had,' he murmured. 'Several times!'

'No, Pip darling, don't set the game up again, once is enough.' Mona's voice broke across them as she restrained her son. 'Anyway, here's Anna coming in to say your supper's ready. Or——?'

'It's the telephone, Madami—for Dr Justin,' Anna told her.

'Oh, I—I didn't hear it. We must have been making too much noise!'

Mona's jump, and then her relaxation on the last words, suggested to Vivien that she had probably thought it was Charles Mantagna ringing her. If she really found him such a nuisance it was surprising she couldn't bring herself to say so; except that Vivien had seen how easily she let herself be bullied by the Mantagnas. Inheriting her late husband's wealth obviously didn't make her life any more comfortable. Justin had got to his feet to follow Anna into the hall and Vivien resisted the temptation to watch him go, bending her head instead to help Philip tidy away the game. He was flushed and triumphant over winning and would probably need restraining from reliving every move over the light supper he was always given before bedtime.

Justin came back before they had got that far. 'I've got to go out,' he said to the room at large. 'Christiane's got a patient she wants me to look at—totally unofficial and purely for my interest, but I said I'd go. You won't mind if I take the car, Mona?'

'No, of course not. Does that mean you won't be in for dinner?'

'Sorry, yes, I said I'd go straight away. Give Tina my apologies in case she's cooked one of my favourites!'

Vivien was just approaching the door with the game box in her hand and Philip in front of her. Justin stood politely out of their way, giving Philip's hair an affectionate ruffle. He was looking exceptionally cheerful. Obviously an evening of Christiane's medical company was a welcome thought. However, as Vivien came up to him feeling suddenly blank inside she felt a light touch on her shoulder and as her eyes jerked to his face she saw that his gaze still held that same look of mixed amusement and challenge.

'*You* owe me a forfeit,' he said silkily. 'I shall have to remember to collect it when I get back, won't I?'

'Oh, I should imagine you'll have forgotten the whole game by then!'

'Don't count on it. Good night, PJ—if you go on showing this much bounce, I should think we'll be able to consider you quite cured any day now! And then,' he added, 'we *will* be able to take that boat trip I promised you. Though this time, I think you'd better sit and watch while I teach Vivien how to use a sailboard rather than learning yourself. No, don't complain—you'll be able to have a good laugh at the number of times she falls off, because beginners always do!'

He didn't wait to see Vivien's reaction to that, but was gone, on a grin. She tried to think resentfully that he hadn't asked her if she wanted to learn to wind-surf, he had simply informed Philip that he would teach her; but the resentment kept getting swallowed up in the oddest feeling of consolation because he had made such a point of it. She pulled herself together and concentrated on Philip, who was already beginning to fizzle at the promised treat. At this rate he would have too much on his mind to be able to settle for the night at all; and she was soon into a firm, 'No, Uncle Justin *didn't* say tomorrow, he said *some time*—and I shall wish he hadn't, if you're going to get so worked up about it!'

Justin hadn't come in by the time Vivien herself went to bed. Perhaps the interesting patient had been followed by an equally interesting and long-drawn-out dinner date. She knew suddenly and with heart-stopping certainty that she *was* jealous . . . however hard she tried to tell herself she wasn't, however much she tried to repeat to herself that she was fireproof where Justin was concerned. She wasn't: she was sinking deeper and deeper into a fascination that sang through her blood. She didn't even want to think about all the reasons why she shouldn't give in to it. All she wanted was to bury hot cheeks in her pillow and dream.

CHAPTER TEN

IN THE morning she made herself decide that sanity was uppermost, and that if she had to be so stupid, at least she needn't show it. She tried not to prick her ears to hear Justin's footsteps and his lighthearted whistle while she was breakfasting with Philip in the boy's room. She refused to wonder when they would run into each other. Then she had to assure herself that she wasn't disappointed when the study door was shut and the tap of the typewriter was coming from behind it by the time she and Philip went downstairs. So he was busy today—why not? It was what he was supposed to have come out here for. It was a pity—no, it was a good thing!—when Mona decided to take Philip out in the car and Vivien with him, so that the two of them could go for a short stroll by the sea in Sliema while Mona did some shopping.

In fact they stayed out to lunch, with Mona suddenly deciding that it was time to emerge from the shelter of her home for once. They went to a smart-looking restaurant—where, nevertheless, the bowing head water who immediately came to serve them didn't turn a hair when Philip demanded hamburger with tomato ketchup—and they hadn't been sitting there long when a chic and much-beringed acquaintance of Mona's swooped down on them from across the room.

'Mona darling! I haven't seen you for ages, where *have* you been hiding yourself? I shall come and join you—I may, mayn't I? Oh, and I see you've got your boy back again . . .'

She spared a smile for Vivien when she was introduced, but then proceeded to chatter on about her husband, her children of whom there seemed to be four or five, and various mutual acquaintances. Her eyes also lit up when she heard that Justin was in Malta.

'Oh, that brother of yours—such a heartbreaker! Of course I haven't seen him for years—but you say he still isn't married? Oh, now that does give me an idea! You remember how keen he used to be on Barbara Pasoli before she married her John? Well, how about getting him together with John's sister Germaine? She's much the same type as Barbara—you know they're all second cousins—and it would be *so* suitable! She's rather independent and studying to be a lawyer, but it's such a good family, of course. We must arrange something!'

Vivien tried to blank out the enthusiastic words, and to counter a sharp dislike for this woman. She took care to keep her eyes on Philip, who was looking bored and somewhat sulky. Mona didn't seem very keen on this friend of hers either, which was perhaps a comfort. However, she was agreeing, vaguely, that Justin might like to take up with some old friends, though Mona herself didn't feel like partying at the moment when her poor little Pip had just been so ill.

'Has he? Oh yes, I believe I heard something from the Mantagnas. When he's your only one it must be such a worry.' The woman cast a sugary look in Philip's direction, but was off again on a eulogy about her own numerous offspring before she could notice the boy's sulky look in return. She went on with, 'You were widowed so young, poor darling, and that wonderful Lewis . . . I can't really believe it was all of six years ago, it still makes me feel terribly sad! But didn't I hear you just *might* marry again into the same family?'

'If you did it was only a rumour!' Mona assured her.

'Oh dear, am I speaking out of turn? But you must know everyone's predicting it, and after all, what could be more reasonable? Mantagna class and Mantagna money—All right, I won't say a word!' She gave a tinkling laugh, cast a conspiratorial look towards Philip, and put one scarlet fingernail to her lips. 'We'll go back to talking about your brother instead. I can think of lots of people, and particularly females, who'd love to see him again! We haven't got that many well-connected bachelors to choose from in our society, now have we? I shall give you a ring and do my best to lure him out!'

The day suddenly seemed unpromising as a rather quiet group made its way back to Valletta. The obvious reference to Charles Mantagna had sent Mona into a state of abstraction, and Philip into a suddenly withdrawn uncertainty that squeezed at Vivien's heart when she saw how white he had gone, and for once without producing a scene. Then he created a diversion by saying he felt sick, and she was immediately worried in case he should start running a temperature again, just now when he had been so much better. The abrupt resentment she had been feeling towards Justin died as she thought thankfully that at least he would be there if Philip was going to produce a recurrence. The same thought was obviously in Mona's mind as they went into the house, and she cast an anxious look at her son and then spoke to Vivien.

'Do you think we stayed out too long? Go upstairs with Vivien, Pip darling, and lie down for a bit—I've just got something I want to talk to Uncle Jus about.'

Vivien half expected Justin to come up, but he didn't. Philip had decided he didn't feel sick any more, but he did agree to have a rest. Once Vivien had checked that he would really settle she left him to it, since it was probably the best thing for him. She hesitated, suddenly unwilling to go downstairs, then lifted her chin and calmed her face and went.

She met Mona coming out of the drawing-room looking even more distracted.

'How's Pip?' asked Mona.

'He seems all right. I think it may only have been car-sickness. Does—does your brother——?'

'Just has gone!' Mona made the announcement in a tone that was halfway between bewilderment and exasperation. 'I wish he'd give some warning, but apparently he had to decide in a hurry. Something about some notes that are missing after all so the only thing he can do is go back and check them at source. So——'

'He's gone back to London?' exclaimed Vivien.

'No, I don't think so,' said Mona, looking faintly surprised as if London hadn't occurred to her. 'Not unless the flight goes that way. He's gone to Riyadh. Apparently his contact at the airport could book him on connecting flights right through to Saudi Arabia if he went straight away. Oh, he left a message about you at the end of the letter he left for me . . . Here it is: "Make sure Vivien stays on, I'll expect her to be still here when I come back, if it runs on over the end of her contract make a further booking.' Is that all right with you, Vivien? I—I would like to know you're here until Pip's completely better, and Jus does make a point of it——'

'I can stay on for as long as you need me.' Vivien wasn't entirely sure she was necessary now, unless Philip was going to produce a recurrence of symptoms, but it seemed to be the only answer she could make. Both her heart and her head told her so, even against her better judgement. 'How—how long will he be away? Does he say?'

'About a week. He also wants to know if I know when Mamma's coming back. I don't know why, when I told him only yesterday I didn't.' A cloud touched Mona's brow for a moment to make her look harassed, and there was an unexpectedly waspish note in her voice as she went on. 'At least if he's swanning off round the world he can escape from anyone's plans to marry *him* off to someone suitable! Though I don't know why I didn't tell Alina Valdi not to get her hopes up: he always does exactly what he likes!'

There was a glitter in her eyes that looked suspiciously

like unshed tears, and a crossness in her voice that brought a sudden reminder of Philip in one of his less tractable moods. Vivien wanted to say something sympathetic, but she knew it was scarcely her business, so she satisfied herself by giving Mona a warm smile with a touch of ruefulness in it. She recieved a tremulous smile in return before Mona swept out of the room without remembering to say anything further about Philip.

Vivien could have agreed, grimly, that Justin obviously did always do exactly what he liked. Such as commanding people to be here when he got back. For what? Her heart gave a thud between anticipation and doubt. For a moment, thinking he had simply taken off back to London, she had felt a sharp stab at the prospect. He would take up where he had left off with Caroline, no matter what he had said about her. Vivien's instant dislike for that thought should have made her feel guilty, but it didn't; it merely made her feel slightly sick and extraordinarily wistful. The fact that she was glad he *hadn't* gone to London could, very promptly, be given the excuse that Caroline was better off without him. She might even have gone back to Tom by now, which was the best thing for all of them. She probably had, since Vivien hadn't heard a word from him, any more than she had ever got round to writing to him . . . which only went to show how unreal the whole thing had been for both of them.

Her muddled thoughts didn't help her own feeling of being heartsore. It didn't help, either, to know that she was busily giving her heart in an entirely untrustworthy direction and was likely to get it broken. The only solution to that was to talk sense into herself during the days Justin was away. She certainly wasn't going to feel that the house felt remarkably empty without him.

It felt emptier than ever during the evening when Mona asked abruptly, with an odd flush in her cheeks,

'Would you mind if I went out for a while? I—I'm sorry about leaving you alone——'

'Of course I don't mind. Please, you don't have to stay in for my benefit—and Philip seems quite all right tonight, in fact he's sleeping so peacefully I think he was just overtired.'

'I don't suppose I'll be late. I just—thanks!'

There was no reason for an employer to apologise for going out, let alone to ask permission—but then Mona never really treated her as if she was an employee. Vivien spent a lonely evening in front of the television watching several imported American cop shows, incomprehensible because they were dubbed into Maltese.

Mostly, however, she brooded wistfully over Justin's absence. People who took planes to the other side of the world as casually as other people took buses really were out of her league. It seemed like a sharp reminder, on top of Alina Valdi's comments on his social eligibility.

She trailed dispiritedly up to bed after looking in on Philip to see that he was still sleeping peacefully and showing no signs of a returning fever. He seemed better in the morning too, if a little listless. Dr Laurens called and didn't seem at all worried, especially as there was no indication of glands or a sore throat. He gave Vivien his usual kindly and approving smile and said he would call again in a few days but he could always be reached sooner if she was at all worried.

Mona seemed to be thoroughly on edge, but insisted that Vivien should be off for the afternoon. She also seemed particularly interested in where she would choose to go—swimming at Sliema, or somewhere else?

'Um—I think I'll go to the Art Museum,' she said. 'It's in the La Valletta Palace, isn't it?'

'That one—oh yes. Don't forget it won't reopen until four. Do go there, I'm sure you'll find it interesting.'

Vivien supposed she would, if Mona so particularly recommend it. It was somewhere to pass the time anyway, and should be cool in the increasing afternoon heat. She duly approached it just after four, paid for a ticket to go in, and wandered round the high marble-pillared rooms wondering why the old portraits had to look so aristocratic that she kept being reminded of Justin in one of his loftier and less likeable moods.

She was staring at a periwigged gentleman who had apparently been a Napoleonic governor when a voice spoke behind her.

'Hi. Mind if I walk round with you?'

The voice was male, amiable, and had the touch of a Geordie accent. As Vivien turned she was struck by a sudden feeling of recognition, though the young man who was smiling at her shouldn't have been familiar. He was as dark as a Maltese in spite of the accent, but had unfashionably long curly hair to his shoulders, and one silver earring. Frayed jeans and a white shirt completed the casual image. She was groping with the sudden impression that she *had* seen that thin face and brown eyes when he spoke again.

'Yes, that's right, I am, if that's what you're thinking. And I was outside, on a motorbike—I followed you in. Before we get our wires crossed, though, this isn't just a pick-up. We've got friends in common. You're Vivien, aren't you?'

'Yes. And you're . . .' The name came suddenly into her mind, however unlikely it seemed. 'You *can't* be Zack Delaney?'

It was only five years since he'd been a pop idol, on television almost every time she'd turned it on: drummer with a group called The Green Underground as they soared into popularity with hit after hit. Then, Vivien remembered, they'd broken up and gone their separate ways—and hadn't Zack Delaney retired from the pop world altogether? She looked at him with her eyes wide, and he grinned at her. He had an extraordinary look of placidity, as if he'd come to terms with who he was and where he was going, and a study of his face showed he was older than she had thought at first; probably thirty-five.

He also seemed quite happy to wait while she stood there and looked him over. After a pause he spoke again.

'OK? I'm a friend of Mona's, and I'll come straight to the point: that's the problem. She wasn't sure about you, but I said it was worth trying. She did think you weren't the type to go to the local press with gossip, though—and you're not, are you?'

'No. But I don't—what's——' Vivien began.

'Come on, let's walk round looking friendly-like, and I'll tell you. You don't have to say you'll help—and as far as I'm concerned you can split the whole thing wide open, only Mona's got herself in a tizz and seems to think she'll be put under so much pressure that we won't stand half a chance. Poor lass.' He spoke tranquilly, and as if the conversation were quite a normal one. 'She's got some right narrow-minded relatives, I can tell you! Have you met any of them?'

'Yes . . . Do you mean the in-laws, particularly?'

'That's right. And her mother, though I gather you haven't run into her yet. I'll tell you what I'm after. I need the chance to get to know young Philip without anyone turning him against me first. So I need to call at the house, casual-like. The object is,' he went on, looking calm and gentle, 'to see if the boy likes me enough to have me for a stepfather. I love Mona and she loves me, but that's not enough when there's a child involved, is it?'

He sounded practical about it, and Vivien warmed to him. Zack Delaney of all people! She remembered swiftly that there had been no talk of his being involved in drugs, or sex scandals, or anything that wasn't exemplary: now that she dredged her mind she could even recall hearing that he was a Catholic and had been a teacher before he joined a band. But what on earth was he doing here? And in love with Mona, and she with him, in a most unlikely twist for that convention-ruled household!

She soon learned more, as Zack strolled through the high rooms beside her explaining in his quiet voice. He seemed to feel she was owed a thorough layout of the situation. He had made what he casually described as 'enough bread to last me a lifetime' and had then given up the music business except for writing a song or two now and again. He was obviously a prudent type, as he mentioned owning a couple of companies. However, he himself preferred to be out of the frenetic public world, so he had bought himself a house on Comino with privacy in mind, and had been living there happily for the past two years. Then, this winter, he had met Mona.

'We wouldn't normally move in the same circles,' he explained. 'It was when there was a lot of charity stuff going on. Band-Aid spin-offs, that kind of thing. We happened to meet and it took off from there. Quietly, though—I like privacy, and she's got all this Maltese society hedging her about. Miners' sons don't count for much here, whatever they may have done since. That's to say, you can talk to 'em, but you certainly don't marry 'em.' He didn't sound much troubled about that, more amused. 'It's a bit like another century—several other centuries? Anyway, that's the set-up. I'm not on the acceptable list when it comes down to the nitty-gritty, and Mona's got all these in-laws breathing down her neck. They've been hinting at her that it's time she married again, but into their world, of course. They've even picked someone out for her, I gather.' There was a touch of grimness in his voice. 'Seen him, have you?'

'Charles Mantagna. I can't think why she doesn't just say *no*, firmly!' said Vivien.

'Oh, it's all to do with money, and trusts, and keeping things in the family. Poor little lass, they've got her so conditioned with their talk about duty that it's not surprising she's torn! And then there's young Philip.' Zack glanced at her. 'He was away in England when Mona and I met, staying with her brother. I was going to have an introduction to the boy over lunch yesterday —just casually, "fancy seeing you again" and all that stuff—but then one of the Social Register popped up and joined you all, so . . . Mona's brother staying in the house lately hasn't helped, either.'

'Hasn't she thought of talking to him? He might be sympathetic——'

'You think so? I know he doesn't like this Charles Mantagna——'

'No, he obviously doesn't!' Vivien agreed.

'All the same, my lady says he has his Maltese side when it comes to the family. I wouldn't know, but according to her he's always run his own life on the line of "entertainment is one thing, who you marry is another". Like I said, it *is* like another century here!' Zack grinned ruefully, but then as if misunderstanding something in Vivien's expression added, 'Of course if you don't want to go against him when he's employing you——'

'Mona employs me. I was just going to say, how do you both feel I can help?'

'We thought maybe . . .' He smiled at her suddenly. 'If it isn't too much to ask, would you care to pretend to be my temporary girlfriend?'

'Oh, I see!' Vivien looked up at him with light dawning. 'You'd call at the house to see me, Mona would kindly suggest you could come whenever you liked, and the Mantagnas might disapprove but they couldn't say much?'

'Ay, just that. Sorry if it doesn't sound very complimentary to ask you to play decoy—but as long as you haven't got anyone else out here who might create, it *would* answer the problem!'

It might answer one of Vivien's own too. If Justin came back to find she had apparently entered on a lighthearted holiday romance, that would make it perfectly clear to him that she'd never taken him at all seriously. The idea struck her with great appeal, even if she still couldn't quite believe she was standing here talking to someone famous enough to have featured in posters pinned to bedroom walls. Zack Delaney would make the perfect decoy from her side too . . . glamorous, definitely attractive in his tall gentle way, someone she might easily have fallen headlong for in anyone's eyes. She opened her mouth to bring out a, 'Yes, OK, I'll do it!' but at the last moment caution intervened.

'I'll have to talk to Mona first.'

''Course. I might be trying to push her in a direction she doesn't really want to go, mightn't I? Or I might have a wife and six kids already—I haven't. Never had time, we were always touring,' Zack said placidly, and eyeing her with friendly approval. 'I'm glad you're being careful—it shows you *are* the sort of girl Mona thinks you are. You talk it all over with her and let us know what you decide. We only decided that I'd discuss it with you first because she didn't quite have the nerve—and besides . . .' he gave her a look somewhere between amusement and apology, 'to make it look real you'll have to be seen with me a bit, and you might not have wanted to agree to that sight unseen!'

He had probably wanted to sum *her* up too, Vivien guessed, aware that there was a great deal of intelligence somewhere behind those tranquil brown eyes. He had been around; he must have had girls screaming after him as well as trying to make something out of being seen with him; he was actually being remarkably trusting in talking to her so directly. She could only feel flattered that he had—and be aware, too, that he could simply have used her without telling her the truth. He wasn't at all what she would have expected of a former pop idol, and she had found him instinctively likeable. She tried to visualise him as a husband for Mona and a stepfather for Philip, and oddly enough it was a picture that seemed to fit together very well. It was easy to imagine his air of tranquillity calming an excitable child . . . and acting as a lovingly secure foil for Mona too. She came out of her thoughts to find he was still watching her placidly, apparently not at all put out by the fact that she was obviously assessing him. She flushed a little, then smiled up at him brilliantly.

'No, I wouldn't mind being seen with you—but I *will* talk to Mona first, right? It all sounds quite—quite possible, so we'll probably only discuss ways and means. Anyway, it's . . . been nice to meet you.'

'And you. Hope we do again.'

His grin answered her own, and when she walked away he didn't try to come with her, merely raised an amiable hand in farewell. Glancing back from the doorway, Vivien saw he was still standing there, looking up at one of the portraits with a thoughtful air as if that was all he had come to the museum for. A bubble of laughter caught at her. *Zack Delaney* of all people . . . and she had just spent an amiable half hour chatting with him, let alone the fact that she might be about to launch herself into pretending to be his girlfriend.

She had to wait until evening to talk things over with Mona, though that lady gave her a look between anxiety and hopefulness when she came in. It was only after Philip was in bed that they could get their heads together. Then Vivien was given a flood of information by a girl who seemed much brighter and less careworn in the relief of having someone she could talk to.

'Vivien, do you think you *could*?' she asked eagerly. 'I know you must think I'm awfully spineless——'

'No, I don't. You just don't want people making a lot of fuss and distressing Philip. I *can* see why you might feel like that!'

'I hoped you would. I do love Zack—I don't see how anybody could help it. He's wonderful . . . but I can't promise to marry him unless Pip likes him,' said Mona, looking tragic all of a sudden, 'and I know they'd all do their best to poison things if I—if we——'

'If you aren't given the chance to sort it out in peace.' What Mona would do if Philip still didn't like Zack was a point neither of them could raise. 'Don't worry,' Vivien told her, with a hidden touch of grim resolution behind her cheerfulness, '*I* don't mind helping to give you that chance! We—we'll just pretend to everybody that Zack's calling round to see me, and that you're being kind enough to encourage it, and let them make what they like out of it! I certainly don't mind helping you to outwit Charles Mantagna, because I can't stand him any more than Philip can—if you'll excuse my saying so!'

Mona's giggle was refreshingly free from apprehension. 'You sounded just like Jus for a minute!' she said, then sobered and added, 'You do understand that I don't want him to know either? It's not that . . . it's just that I can't be sure . . .'

'Oh, I agree! It ought to be a completely private arrangement! Just you, me, and Zack.'

For a moment Vivien wondered if she had sounded too emphatic or answered too fast. Mona didn't seem to notice. She was giving Vivien such a look of relief and gratitude that it was almost enough to make her feel guilty; and she obviously didn't have the faintest idea that her son's nurse might have reasons of her own for wanting Justin kept out of the secret.

CHAPTER ELEVEN

'SURE I'll teach you how to play the drums, if your mum doesn't mind,' Zack said tranquilly. 'You'll need a practice pad, though—that's a thing with a rubber top so that you can try out rhythms on it without making a noise. It's the best way to learn without driving everyone mad.'

He and Philip were getting on like a house on fire. They had from the start. Zack's easy manner and his habit of treating the boy with exactly the same attention as he gave everyone else, no more and no less, seemed to work wonders. He was obviously used to children, liked them, and believed in treating them in the same reasonable manner he would offer to an adult.

Vivien had been out on the back of his motorbike by prearrangement and everyone knew that she had brought him back to the house and asked him if he'd mind showing the gleaming metal monster to her charge. It had made a perfect introduction as well as providing Mona with the perfect excuse for remembering she had met him before and inviting him in, as a thank-you for his patience in demonstrating the bike to her son and explaining all its parts to him. It was all so innocently public that no one could have thought twice about it—let alone the fact that Zack's preference for a motorbike over a car inevitably sent him up several notches in a ten-year-old's estimation. Philip had even accepted with remarkably good grace Zack's refusal to take him as a pillion passenger with a calm but firm, 'I never give rides to anyone under sixteen, sorry!'

There had been another piece of unexpected publicity which had been disconcerting for a moment. Vivien had been out with him for an evening as part of the false trail. She hadn't been quite sure that it was necessary and had felt awkward about it, except that he was easy company and took the whole thing with an amused relaxation—but she hadn't been prepared for a flashbulb going off in her face just as they left a restaurant on their way to a cinema.

'I still rate local news, do I? No, we don't want to say anything—come on, Vivien!'

Zack had been holding the door open for her and she had been glancing back up at him to say something. Now he caught hold of her quickly to whisk her away and Vivien couldn't help wondering, as the flashbulb exploded again, whether the second photograph would show them looking startled and furtive as they fled. Hand in hand. She supposed it was all to the good, though when she glanced at Zack he was frowning a little and looking rueful.

'I didn't stage that, actually. They must be having a slow news week for gossip. Do you mind?'

'No, why should I? Anyway—'she laughed at him—'I'm only human, you know, so if they print it I'll probably cut it out and keep it as a souvenir!'

She was glad when he chuckled at that. 'OK, I'll even sign it—if you really want a piece of dead history! Be warned, though, if they're really out to fill a bit of space they'll probably describe us as "dining tête-à-tête and staring lovingly into each other's eyes"!' He gave her a grin with a shrug and a, 'That's the way it goes!'

He was an extraordinarily comfortable man to be with, quiet and unruffled and intelligent, and they had actually spent the meal talking about their respective families with an ease that conquered Vivien's initial shyness. His was apparently large, urban and sprawling, made up of nieces and nephews, uncles and aunties, grandparents, innumerable cousins. He was one of six which, he said with amusement, ensured that he 'kept his head screwed on'. He seemed thoroughly lacking in conceit, and Vivien's initial instinctive liking for him increased the more she saw him. It really wouldn't be all that difficult to pretend to be in a starry-eyed state when Justin came back . . .

She wished wistfully that she could imagine him being jealous. *Genuinely* jealous. It was part of the dream she carried around with her, along with wondering where he was now, what he was doing, what he was thinking and feeling, how he was looking. She tried hard not to think about him at all, but that only brought him to haunt her dreams. She would wake heavy-eyed and then tell herself defiantly that what she was doing now was all to the good; it was helpful to Mona and a defence for herself.

'Mummy, can I have a practice pad?' Philip asked excitedly, bringing Vivien back to the present with a jerk. 'I can, can't I?'

'Yes, darling, I should think so, if Zack would really be kind enough—' Mona wasn't a very good actress, and to Vivien the way she looked at Zack was all too revealing. Philip didn't seem to notice it. 'I expect we can buy one somewhere.'

'Tell you what before you do that—when you're well enough for a day out you can come over to my house and try one out there,' suggested Zack. 'You might like my house anyway. You and your mum and Vivien could all come over for the day.'

'And Uncle Justin? He's been promising to take me over to Comino.'

'Your Uncle Justin too if he wants to come,' said Zack without a flicker, ignoring the way Mona had coloured up and was casting him a look of alarm. 'Why not? He'd be welcome. He'll be back before too long, I gather, so——'

'Oh, I should think he'll be too busy. And Pip, you shouldn't add other people on when people give you an invitation, it isn't polite. I'm sure Justin won't——'

'Justin won't what?' a voice asked from the doorway. A cool, conversational, and very familiar voice, sending Vivien's heart jerking into her throat.

She hadn't heard the door open—none of them had. He wasn't due back until tomorrow at the earliest. If they hadn't all been out in the courtyard, with a large striped umbrella erected to protect them from the late afternoon sun, they might have heard the sounds of someone at the front door . . . For a moment she scarcely dared to look round, so that by the time she did Zack had already turned his head tranquilly and both the others had broken into speech.

'Oh, Jus, you did give me a start!'

'Vivien's friend Zack says we can go over and visit him on Comino——'

'And this is Vivien's friend Zack?'

There was nothing to be heard in his voice besides politeness. There was nothing in his face either as he gave a nod to the other man and he wasn't bothering to cast so much as a glance at Vivien. She might have been invisible. His eyes were narrowed against the sunlight and there were tired lines round his mouth, but otherwise he simply looked faintly bored. Vivien's heart turned over nevertheless at the sight of him. She tried to convince herself that it was merely a reflex action, because he certainly wasn't looking particularly lovable.

'Forgive me if I don't do more than say hello, but I've been flying far too long and I need a shower and a change of clothes. Is all well with you, PJ? You look healthy enough, I must say!'

'He's much better, Jus, truly. Dr Laurens is very pleased with him. I didn't think you'd be back until——'

'If I'd known seeing me was going to put an expression like that on your face, perhaps I wouldn't have hurried back,' retorted Justin, regarding his sister with irritation. 'I said I was coming back, does it have to make you look as if you're going into heart failure? If so, I'd better get out of your way!'

The rough edge on his voice obviously had nothing to do with Vivien since he still didn't acknowledge her, merely gave another nod in Zack's direction and disappeared into the house. So much for dreams. Philip opened his mouth with an air of grievance that his uncle hadn't stayed to listen when he had something he wanted to say, but at that moment Anna appeared.

'Mr Mantagna is here, Madami. I've put him in the drawing-room.'

'He is? Oh—oh yes, I'd forgotten it's one of his usual days. I'll—I'll come in and see him, thank you, Anna. Pip darling, you stay out here with Vivien and Zack and—and—'

Mona didn't finish her sentence but came to her feet in a swirl of skirts and hurried into the house. Knowing how visible they must be from the drawing-room windows, Vivien wondered if she was supposed to make some obvious gesture—though she'd hardly be expected to be holding Zack's hand in front of Philip, surely? A bubble of hysterical laughter suddenly caught at her as she visualised herself bounding across to sit on his knee. It would be better, perhaps, to look as if she was making bright conversation—however little she felt like it just at the moment . . .

Then she forgot artifice as raised voices abruptly floated out through the drawing-room windows. The words weren't audible, but the tones indicated a quarrel going on, and Zack had tensed and was looking exactly as if he was about to launch into a protective raid. Vivien leaned forward swiftly and laid a hand on his arm, at the same time as she launched into bright speech.

'Philip love, if you bang your fingers on the table that hard you'll bruise yourself. Why don't you try beating out a rhythm on a cushion instead? Zack can tell you if you're doing it right. I'm just going to pop indoors and——'

'You're just trying to stop me listening to Mummy shouting at Uncle Charles. I'm glad if she is—I hate him!'

'All the more reason to bang a cushion,' said Vivien on an attempted laugh, to lighten the whole thing into a joke. She added hastily, 'But I don't think you should really say things like that, it's—um—not really terribly polite, is it?' She came to her feet, and tried to look as if her hand on Zack's shoulder was merely a way of pulling herself up rather than a physical pressure to keep him in his seat. He must surely see that this wasn't a moment to bring things to a head, with Philip in the middle of it. 'I won't be a minute, there's just something I want to fetch out of the drawing room.'

She was giving his shoulder another warning squeeze as she spoke, and intending to convey that it was better if *she* interrupted than he did, and it would have the effect of deflecting Charles Mantagna's criticisms on to her anyway. He cast her a swift upward glance, raised a hand to touch hers in acknowlgedement, and began to turn back to Philip with an immediate, 'Here, throw us that cushion next to you and I'll show you, like Vivien says—'

Vivien didn't know what made her glance up at the house as she turned away from them. Justin had obviously just been pushing his windows wide and she caught a flash of movement as he moved out of view. She had forgotten his room looked this way. It was illogical to wish it didn't, that she wasn't putting up a pretence to him as well as to the Mantagnas, when she had quite deliberately wanted it to be so. Thoroughly illogical, when he obviously didn't care either way.

But then love wasn't logical: it was confused, and painful, and weakened every resolution she ever tried to make.

Her intention to interrupt Mona and Charles Mantagna wasn't necessary, because she had only reached the courtyard door when it was pulled open and Mona appeared looking flushed and angry. Charles could be seen across the hall behind her, leaving stiffly. If Mona had learned how to oust him that was all to the good, even if nothing else was.

Vivien had to wait until later, after Zack had left, to find out what the quarrel had actually been about. Mona swept them all into the house on the excuse that Philip had had enough sun for today, and Anna was about to bring them cool drinks indoors. It might only have been Vivien who was aware that she also cast a swift wary glance of her own up at Justin's open window. He hadn't reappeared when Zack departed with Mona saying clearly in the hall, 'Do come and see Vivien again tomorrow!' with a dimpling smile and a loving look which Philip would certainly have noticed, if Anna hadn't already taken him off to give him his early supper. Since there was no one else about Vivien ran upstairs quickly to her room so that they had a chance to say goodbye properly—and was all too aware of Justin's closed door opposite her own.

She hadn't got far with some very unproductive thoughts before a tap on her door heralded Mona. The other girl was looking shiny-eyed as she closed the door behind her, but there was anxiety overlying it.

'Vivien——'

'Is there a problem?'

'Not really, apart from Jus turning up when I wasn't expecting him! I can't decide whether he wasn't in the best of moods because Zack was here or for some reason of his own. Still, he can't really object to your friends, can he?' Mona plumped down on the edge of the bed beside Vivien. 'And I did manage to send Charles off with a flea in his ear by losing my temper with him for interfering, instead of trying to argue!' Her expression held surprise as well as satisfaction that the tactic had worked. 'He was on about you—wanting me to send you home. That picture of you and Zack has just come out in this week's paper.'

'Oh—oh, has it? I didn't know.'

'Well, it's recognisably you, apparently, and besides, it gives your first name. Charles calls it "undesirable publicity".' A giggle broke through, though a moment later Mona had sobered again. 'That's not the trouble, though, it's actually working out quite well. It's just that Charles also made the point that you're not necessary any more now that Pip's so much better, and that's a harder one to answer—particularly now Jus is back so that I haven't got the excuse of saying I must keep you on because he said so. So I wanted to say, you won't leave yet, will you? No matter what anyone says?'

'I was just wondering how long you did need me for, as a matter of fact,' Vivien admitted. 'Philip obviously does like Zack——'

'Yes, but I want to give it a bit longer.' Mona reached for Vivien's hands with a look of entreaty. 'Particularly now Jus is going to be in the house! Please promise me you'll stay, even if *he* says anything to you!'

'Well, all right——'

'Oh, thank you!' said Mona, jumping up, and added, 'It's going to be hard enough to keep away from his sharp eyes as it is. And—and if that worries you, I promise I'll tell him afterwards that I got you to lie for me, in case you're afraid that he might not give you any more jobs or something!'

'I'm not. I don't always do private nursing—and I'll probably look for a hospital job again when I get back to England. So there's no need to tell him anything,' said Vivien.

'You're a darling to be so helpful,' Mona told her in heartfelt tones, and flitted away looking satisfied. Vivien went back to her brooding.

It was like an itch to want to see Justin. She did, briefly, when she came out of her room just as he was coming out of his. Her heart performed its usual antics and before she could stop herself she had asked quickly,

'Did you manage to find the missing notes you went for?'

'Yes, thank you. It wasn't all that hard. I should be able to get on with things properly now, without interruptions!'

The unsmiling look he was giving her suggested he was classing her among the interruptions. Vivien felt a spark of anger, but he had turned on his heel and was walking away.

Philip scarcely needed seeing to bed now he was well, and his chief desire was for Uncle Justin to come and say good night to him. Uncle Justin did, and Vivien closed the door sharply on a conversation all about 'Vivien's friend Zack who used to play drums in a band' and graphic details about Zack's motorbike. If there was one thing Philip liked it was being able to pass on information about whatever was intriguing him most at the moment. He was, of course, playing beautifully into his mother's hands . . . and into Vivien's she told herself quickly. And it didn't really matter that Justin seemed to have lost the least desire to charm her during his week's absence—as long as he realised that she hadn't spared him a thought all the time he'd been away!

Perhaps he had met an old flame in Riyadh and regretted having to come back to Malta. It was a pity from everyone's point of view that he had. Vivien felt an urgent need to go home. Unfortunately she couldn't, when she had just promised Mona she would stay.

She went down to dinner wearing a deliberately bright expression as befitting someone who was supposed to be in the throes of an exciting new relationship, only to find Justin wasn't down yet so the expression was wasted. Mona was, but she had just begun a conspiratorial smile when Justin arrived with a soft-footed grace that made his sister jump guiltily. He didn't seem to notice it, but went to pour himself a whisky, throwing a comment back over his shoulder.

'Anna tells me Alina Valdi's been ringing me. Something about a dinner party she wants to fix up. I must ring her back—I suppose it's about time I picked up with a few people.'

'Oh yes, she said something about wanting to see you when I met her. You ought to go, Jus. I told her *I* wouldn't, because of Pip——'

'He's scarcely an excuse to keep you in now. In fact he doesn't actually need—' He turned his head as Anna appeared in the doorway. 'Are we being summoned in to eat already? I'll have to take my whisky in with me, then.'

'No, Dr Justin, it's the telephone for Miss. An overseas call from a Dr Ainslie,' Anna said helpfully to Vivien, 'and he's holding on, if Miss would like to come?'

This time it was Vivien's turn to jump guiltily, and she scrambled to her feet, thoroughly aware of Justin's raised eyebrows and sardonic gaze. She was too busy feeling surprised that Tom should ring her all the way from England—or Scotland—to wait for the comment which was obviously hovering on Justin's lips, and she was glad to see Anna pulling the door firmly closed behind her as Vivien sped to pick up the receiver lying off the hook on the table in the hall.

'Tom? Why are you—Look, I'm sorry I haven't written, but——'

'It's all right, Viv. Well, it is and it isn't, but I'm feeling rather bad about things, so I thought I'd better actually talk to you.' He sounded as near as if he was in the next room. 'Look, it's like this. Caroline and I——'

'If you're back together again I'm absolutely delighted,' Vivien said swiftly, to clear the faint tinge of guilt in his voice. 'I couldn't be more pleased. *Are* you?'

'Well, yes. And in view of—of certain things I said——'

'Don't be silly. We were both just—Well, you know and I know. Is Caroline with you?'

'No, not just at the moment. I haven't told her that . . . I said there was *someone*, just so that she wouldn't have things all her own way, but I didn't say who. I shan't either, unless you want me to. Viv——'

'Don't worry about it, Tom. I'm having an absolutely marvellous time out here,' Vivien said mendaciously, 'and I'm afraid I haven't thought about you since I arrived. Sorry, love, though it's just as well, isn't it? How *is* Caroline? Is she OK? I mean——'

'She's fine, and she says she woke up one morning to realise that she'd just been suffering from a temporary aberration which wasn't at all real. She's also admitted that it was her doing all the chasing, so I suppose I don't have to find the bastard in question and knock his block off,' said Tom, sounding extremely cheerful about it. 'Anyway, I'm going to be around from now on, so he'd better not try and take up where he left off. The Edinburgh job's finished, and as soon as I find another locum we're going to get married. If I'd been there to keep an eye on her none of this would have happened in the first place—Oh. Sorry, that could have been better put!'

'It's quite all right. I'm used to you two, aren't I? And I truly am very pleased for both of you,' Vivien said rapidly, as a distant whistle that might be a time-check sounded somewhere along the line. 'Say you just rang me up to tell me you're engaged and to find out when I'm coming back—though I don't know yet—and give her my love!'

He clicked off the line straight after that, so it must have been a time-check. It had been nice of him to be conscience-stricken enough to phone her. She was delighted to hear that Caroline wasn't still pining for Justin, too. One of them was quite enough. In fact more than enough. Vivien set her chin at a carefully cheerful angle and went back into the drawing-room smiling.

'That was a friend of mine,' she said brightly to Mona's curious face, Justin's sardonic one. 'I hope you didn't mind his ringing, but he wanted to get hold of me urgently because——'

'Your picture's been beamed across the world as well as appearing here?' enquired Justin silkily. Vivien saw he had the local paper in his hand. It hadn't been in the house earlier and she supposed Charles Mantagna must have brought it with him. 'Did you manage to find an excuse? Or did you just tell him to put up with it?'

'I didn't need an excuse. It was a celebration call to tell me that he and my flatmate have just got engaged.' Vivien addressed the words to Mona to stop the sudden flash of guilty worry in her eyes. 'They'd been going around together for ages,' she went on airily, 'when someone came between them, but luckily they've got over that now. Caroline—my friend—says the man who came between them was just a temporary aberration on her part and it was never at all real. I must say I thought so, he did look the type to play fast and loose, and not at all trustworthy!'

'Goodness, how awful for her!' exclaimed Mona, apparently feeling Vivien's sudden stop required some sort of answer. 'But she's got her fiancé back now? I'm not surprised they wanted to ring you up and reassure you it'd all come out right in the end.'

'Yes, it did. And if the other man ever turns up again Tom will knock his block off,' Vivien said sweetly, smiled at Justin, and was annoyed to see that he wasn't looking at all crushed, merely politely interested.

'Fascinating,' he murmured, sounding just like Mr Spock out of *Star Trek*. 'I think I met your friend, didn't

I? The very pretty one? You must give her my best wishes next time you're in touch with her. How lucky she came to her senses!'

'Yes, isn't it? I certainly hoped she would!'

'Friendship can do no less. You did say it was only one person who came between them—not someone on both sides?'

'I don't know why you're taking so much interest in all this, Jus,' Mona broke in. 'You usually say other people's love affairs are so boring!' She seemed puzzled and a little unnerved by the undercurrents swirling round the room.

'I must have mellowed,' her brother retorted blandly. He let the newspaper fall from his hand and raised his glass to Vivien. 'To all loves old and new, serious and unserious—is that a suitable toast? Or would you rather I simply said, To past, present and future?'

There was a gleam in his eye and a glint of mockery. Mona, however, had jumped to her feet as if the conversation was getting too near to home.

'I'm sure we'll all drink to that, even though I don't know the people concerned. Jus, did I tell you that the Mantagnas are having a memorial service for Lewis's grandfather next week? Charles mentioned it when he came round today, it's an evening one in the Cathedral. I suppose you won't want to come . . . No, you didn't really know him, did you? They're bound to say that I ought to bring Pip, but I shan't, it'll be much too long and mournful for him.'

'Quite. You can leave him at home, with Vivien to babysit. I expect she can spare the time, however busy her social life's grown!'

The tone was purely pleasant even if the words were pointed. Vivien wasn't given the chance to answer, because at that moment dinner was announced, and Justin had swung the conversation on to something quite different as they moved to the dining-room to eat.

CHAPTER TWELVE

JUSTIN might have said he didn't want his work interrupted, but that didn't stop him wandering into the drawing-room the next day during Zack's afternoon visit. Mona wasn't there, because Justin's presence in the house had made her decide to be obviously absent. Vivien was busy cutting out the figures for a cardboard theatre Zack had brought as an amusement for Philip, and the other two were working out how to construct proscenium arch and backing from instructions which had been printed in Italian without a translation. Nothing could have been pleasanter than Justin's manner and he must have heard Zack's arrival from the study, since he didn't look at all surprised but merely raised an eyebrow.

'You're getting spoiled for company, PJ. What's that you're making?'

'A theatre, Zack brought it, it cuts out of a book. I'm *not* spoiled,' Philip added automatically, though it came out without any of the animosity he usually showed towards that word.

'I didn't mean it that way, I was just commenting on your luck. You certainly don't look like someone who needs nursing any more, so make the most of it while you've got it!'

'Mummy says Vivien deserves a holiday. Anyway, she can go on being with me because it's not worth my going back to school this term. And it's not,' Philip began warily, looking up at his uncle with the suspicion of the beginning of a jutting lower lip in his old fashion, 'because I *have* been ill, and——'

'Give us that bit, Phil, I've just found out where it

goes,' Zack intervened calmly. If Vivien hadn't seen it happen before she might have been surprised to find Philip dropping rebellion instantly to do as Zack asked. 'Look, it slots in there. Or does it?'

'It might go the other way round?'

'Don't think so, or that tassel would be upside down. I suppose you don't read Italian?' Zack asked Justin pleasantly.

'Not one of my skills, I'm afraid. You seem to have got your working party well organised.' Justin turned his head to look at Vivien sitting silently nearby on the floor. She dropped her eyes rapidly to go on with her cutting out, telling herself that she hadn't been watching him. 'Occupational therapy rather than nursing skills?' his voice enquired above her head.

'Occupational therapy can be part of nursing skills. It's probably classified under social work.' Vivien made her tone as lightly affable as his own, and slanted a quick glance at him under her lashes to prove that it didn't disturb her at all that he had moved to stand over her. Unfortunately it did, so she widened her eyes into an innocently friendly gaze. 'I certainly don't feel as if I'm wasting my time, and besides, Malta's much too lovely to leave before I have to.'

'I've always thought so, though one must, in the end. Where's Mona this afternoon?' he added, looking round as if he almost expected to see her behind one of the sofas.

'She's gone for a walk.'

'How unusual of her. Or unusually tactful? I wanted a word with her, but no doubt I'll see her later. Meanwhile I suppose I'd better not disturb you all, so I'll take myself off back to work.'

'I hope it's going well,' Vivien told him politely, more out of a desire not to let him get the last word than anything. He obviously had only wanted to see Mona; he hadn't come in to check up on her and Zack; or if the latter, only on his nephew's behalf. He had also been doing rather more than hint that for his part he felt it was time she went home. The pang that gave her was so irritating that she almost missed his answer.

'Reasonably, thanks. Now I really have got all the information I'll hope to be finished soon, and able to concentrate on other things. Oh, isn't that Harlequin character you're cutting out supposed to have two arms? I hope it's not my fault for distracting you, but you seem to have chopped one of them off! Never mind, I'm sure it'll mend!'

He didn't have to sound so sympathetic when there was a gleam of amusement in the eyes looking down at her, and neither did he need to walk away immediately so that she didn't have a chance to answer. Vivien glared at his departing back view—was suddenly aware of Zack's eyes resting on her thoughtfully, and was then grateful for Philip's immediate outrage that she had damaged one of his figures, because it gave her a chance to calm down. By the time she had convinced him that it would mend and only needed a bit of Sellotape her heart-rate was more or less back to normal. At least she told herself so.

Justin was out for dinner. Perhaps that was what he had wanted to see Mona about. He was out the following night too, and Vivien had the chance to see him go, looking smooth and smart so that she could see he was going somewhere formal. He was apparently going back upstairs for something he had forgotten, and he stood aside for her as she came down them with a paperback in her hand which she had intended to spend the evening hiding behind in apparent absorption—and as he glanced at it she hoped he noticed it was a biography of Jimi Hendrix, since she had chosen it particularly to show how interested she was in anyone who played in a band.

'Not going out?' he enquired in a tone of polite

sympathy. 'Ah well, I suppose your admirer does have to go back to his island occasionally.'

'It's easier for him to come over during the day,' she explained. 'Besides, Mona might want to go out and visit friends, and as I do still work for her——'

'You don't want to stretch her tolerance too far? I'm glad to hear it. I'm also glad if she's starting to go out again—now that PJ's so much better one can barely even call him convalescent!'

There it was again, the suggestion that Vivien was outstaying her welcome. He had passed her to run lightly upstairs before she could frame an answer which ought only to have been agreement. At that moment she was wishing she had never come; in spite of the beauty of the island which still exerted its fascination over her whenever she went out into it.

She went out on Sunday, the in-laws' visiting day, because Mona seemed to feel it was better if she did even though she was also going to have a whole day off on Tuesday. That was because Zack had some people he must see on that day and his absence coinciding with Vivien's would look as if she was spending the day with him. She took herself down to Marsaxlokk, the fishing village in the south of the island where a whole fleet of the painted *luzzu* could be seen, and found it also had a Sunday fish-market with an enormous variety of the fresh catch to be seen, including giant turtles kept live in a pond until someone wanted to buy them for soup. It was an enchantingly pretty place, and one could also swim from the rocks the other side of its curving bay. Vivien did, and it ought to have been distinctly consoling to find her attention being vied for by two Maltese boys who obviously thought a solitary girl with long black hair and a bikini showing off a golden tan really must want company; and then by a solitary young German tourist who moved in on her with much the same idea.

She did go and have a drink with the German at one of

the quayside cafés, knowing it was idiotic of her not to want to bother because he wasn't Justin. In fact she couldn't even give him her Valletta address when she was supposed to be so wrapped up in Zack. Life was full of complications. She told him she wouldn't be here for more than a few more days and was aware of disappointment in his eyes as she went off to catch her bus. Then she immediately forgot him in the abrupt idea that she might, actually, be sent summarily home. If Justin had been in today and had backed up Mantagna demands for her removal, Mona would have found it hard to think up any excuse.

He hadn't, because he hadn't been in. Mona said he had gone out to spend the day with the Pasolis. Her in-laws had had their usual unnerving effect on her and now (with Philip safely in bed) she was working herself into a fret about Tuesday.

'I'd clean forgotten about the memorial service. Oh, *why* does it have to fall on the same day? Just when I'd carefully made it clear to Jus that you were having that day off to spend with Zack!'

'It can't matter, surely? He won't know, and I could be anywhere, and come back early.' Looking regretful, Vivien thought, trying not to feel sour about it. She didn't suppose Justin had been making any particular enquiry and Mona had probably been overdoing it. 'What time have you got to leave for the service?'

'Six, I suppose. And I made such a point of saying that Pip wasn't quite well enough to go, and that you were still needed to look after him, that——'

'Six is a perfectly reasonable time for me to be back. I needn't go to the Blue Grotto, after all—it was only because it was suitably far away. I'll just keep myself out of sight somewhere nearer, that's all!' Vivien smiled at Mona, trying not to feel that the plotting was growing wearying, and added, 'Zack's going to meet Philip and me at the War Museum tomorrow, isn't he? They really do get on tremendously well, those two, and I've never known anyone so patient at answering questions.'

That was enough to send Mona into a besotted state until the slam of the front door suggested Justin had come back. Vivien decided abruptly that she would go to bed, and went, taking care to give him a bright, 'Good night!' as she passed him, and turn it into a yawn. That way, she didn't have to put up with any solicitous enquiry as to whether she had had a pleasant day, or hear how much he had enjoyed his own.

She had thought the visit to the War Museum which Philip had demanded as an outing would be boring. Instead she found it both sobering and moving, with its grainy photographs showing the terrible devastation this small island had so proudly suffered and survived. All the same she was quite glad to emerge into sunlight and the present, unable to blank out the memory of Justin's voice saying, 'Recent history, here . . .', aware that the older people she met so cheerfully on buses or in shops had actually lived through that. Philip, of course, was full of his usual bounce as they strolled to find a café so that he could have the Coke he had demanded.

'If I'd been alive then I'd have flown one of those planes from Hal Far. I'd have shot down everything that came over. From a plane like that one in there—it was one of the real three, you know!'

'What was left of it. I can't say I go for wars much,' Zack answered him contemplatively, and Vivien was amused to see Philip immediately adjusting his viewpoint like a small admiring shadow.

'No, they're too dev-devastating, even if Malta did have to fight that time. Gozo didn't get bombed so much, but Malta did because they were trying to hit the dockyard. We did it in history at school.'

'That's the thing about studying history, they say —saves you repeating it. Vivien, what would you like —coffee, orange, Coke like Phil? And an ice?'

'Just coffee, thank you.'

She was wondering suddenly whether another photographer would bob up, to annoy the Mantagnas further by showing Philip as well as herself in Zack's company, but nobody seemed to be taking any notice of them in this busy tourist café. Sun-reddened faces and cameras slung round necks showed that the tourist season was thoroughly under way. Vivien couldn't help thinking that she and Zack, both dark-haired and tanned, probably looked like resident Maltese to the visitors. The thought sent her mind off on a drift which was all mixed up with the tap of Justin at the typewriter as she and Philip had left the house; the rigid conventions of Malta's upper society; the wry acknowledgement that she even more than Zack was an outsider. It didn't bother him, but then he had enough to offer so that it needn't. Of course, she added quickly, it didn't bother her either. Not in the least. One of these days she would look back on coming to work out here as nothing but a pleasant and lively memory of hot sun and silkily-warm sea and gracious golden buildings, and nothing else to make her heart stupidly wistful at all . . .

'Never nag a lady, Phil, and you can see she was miles away!' Zack's voice jerked her out of her thoughts and she was suddenly aware that two pairs of eyes were fixed on her, Philip's round ones slightly accusing. 'We were talking about setting a date for that visit to Comino,' Zack explained, his glance deadpan. 'Later this week, perhaps? If it suits Phil's mum, of course.'

'Oh—oh yes, fine! Sorry——'

'Looking at all that wartime stuff's enough to send anyone quiet. Your coffee's getting cold, or do you like it that way?' Zack's smile was as tranquil as usual, but the thoughtfulness with which he was regarding her made her glad he had provided an excuse for whatever her face might have been showing. Vivien brightened deliberately and she made an effort to seem as excited as

Philip about the promised day out at Zack's house —which would, of course, be fun.

Particularly if Justin didn't come too so that they could all relax and stop acting. Vivien couldn't help thinking that Philip was bound to notice shortly just how much his mother liked Zack. She couldn't help thinking too that he would be absolutely delighted, considering the way he had taken to this tall, quiet man.

Meanwhile they had to keep up the fiction that she would be seeing Zack tomorrow, and she was glad if a little surprised to see Philip swallow that with a careful lack of complaint as they parted outside the house some half an hour later. He didn't complain when Zack refused to come in too, and was so obviously taking care not to seem spoiled and over-demanding that it was almost painful. It was like watching him grow up between one minute and the next.

Justin worked all through the afternoon and only emerged from the study to go out, yet again, in the evening. He was obviously picking up with old friends with great enthusiasm. That suited Mona because she could retire to her bedroom and talk on the telephone extension up there without rousing even the most casual interest as to whom she had been ringing for so long. Vivien got out her map of Malta and the bus timetable and tried to find somewhere suitable to go to next day.

She decided on Mellieha Bay, simply because it was far enough away, near enough to get back from, and was marked as having a sandy beach, which was unusual for Malta's rocky coast. It was in the north, too, on the way to the Gozo ferry, and she hadn't been up that way. She couldn't help remembering Justin's offer to take her across to Gozo for the trotting races . . . She tried to blot that out of her mind, but as she slipped out of the house after breakfast next morning without seeing any of the household except Anna, there were too many comparisons to be made with the day when she had set off early

of their seats to thud against each other, against the metal seat-supports, against the floor with a bruising impact. Something crashed and crunched against the radiator with a sudden fierce hiss of steam; something tore and thumped against the back. They were sliding, bumping . . .

Then suddenly they were still.

It had seemed impossible that they wouldn't go over the edge to bounce and tumble towards the sea below. But they hadn't: as Vivien raised her head shakily she found they were still on the road, sideways on and blocking it. The bus, miraculously, was even still on its four wheels. Its engine had died into silence and for a moment there seemed to be no sound but gasps and soft cries and then a clamour as people began to pick themselves up. Voices were raised in fear and shock and indignation, someone was sobbing, and someone else was sending up a quick jabber that sounded like a thankful prayer. Then there were rapidly running feet outside as people emerged from small shops and hotels set above the bay.

Someone pulled Vivien to her feet and patted her anxiously. The driver, white-faced, was staggering out of his seat, with hands reaching out to touch him in congratulation and thankfulness.

Incredibly, as the mêlée sorted itself out, no one seemed to be badly hurt. Vivien winced against a bruise where she had been thrown to the floor, but the passengers were starting to scramble out through the emergency exit at the rear pulled open by helpful hands from outside. There was even shaky laughter as someone cracked what was obviously a joke. Then, just as Vivien was beginning to move in her turn on unsteady legs along the emptying bus, there was a sudden urgent cry from behind her, accompanied by a bitten-off moan.

She turned quickly, training reasserting itself over her dazed shock. 'I'm a nurse,' she said quickly to the person just behind her, squeezing back past him, 'there's someone back there—Please let me through, I'm a nurse, I might be able to help.'

Her words were heard and understood and brought another urgent cry. A young man's white face appeared above one of the seats. He caught Vivien's searching gaze and beckoned desperately. 'Nurse? Please? My wife—*please*!'

Even before she reached them Vivien had remembered the heavily-pregnant girl, with a jolt of guilt that she should have forgotten. The girl's husband must have lifted her back on to her seat and she was huddled there with her hands curled protectively and despairingly round her swollen abdomen. Her face was white and frightened and sheened with sweat, and her bottom lip showed a fleck of blood where it was caught between her teeth.

Vivien knelt down beside her quickly. Even as she did so, the girl let out another sharp moan. There was an abrupt flood of clear liquid gushing out to soak the seat beneath her and drip on to the floor. Her hand reached out to grip Vivien's convulsively, and her eyes were full of a terrified appeal.

Her waters had broken, and it was obvious that the baby might be born any minute.

CHAPTER THIRTEEN

AFTERWARDS Vivien wondered how she had kept so cool.

Afterwards she had time to feel all sorts of things: relief that it wasn't the girl's first baby, because that might have been harder, thankfulness that she *had* once delivered a baby when everyone expected her to know what to do, an even greater thankfulness when an ambulance arrived only moments after she had wrapped a small, slippery infant, still attached to cord and placenta, in the clean towel someone thrust at her. Very much a live baby, thank God, who seemed remarkably none the worse for having been born unexpectedly on a crashed bus.

Vivien went along in the ambulance to make sure of that. She was swept by a fierce protectiveness for the tiny life she had helped to deliver, and no one questioned that she should go too. She was sped on her way by an embarrassing amount of congratulations, a wave of goodwill, people smiling and touching her almost as if she had acted as a talisman. She knew she had really done nothing except be there—but the new baby girl's young parents were embarrassing in their gratitude, and a hastily summoned mother-in-law flung her arms round Vivien in a tearful embrace. That had been later, at the hospital, where Vivien had waited to make sure everything was really all right with both mother and child. By the time she left she had been flooded with open invitations to visit them—any time, any year, whenever she wanted to come to Malta.

She was driven home by a police escort, and the chatty and admiring driver seemed more than inclined to suggest a date some time. 'Are you staying long on the island? Do you have much free time? You're from London, eh? I've got an uncle in Slough, that's not far from London, is it? Maybe one of these days I'll be over to visit him.'

'I hope you enjoy it if you do. You'll miss all your lovely sunshine, though!' Vivien shivered a little as her euphoria began to wear off, and added, 'Do you often get bus crashes like that?'

'It happens. Some car driver gets careless—or rash! Lucky there weren't any broken arms and legs this time,' he said cheerfully. 'Some of our boys will be up there winching the bus round to get it off the road and taking details. I expect they'll have the traffic moving again by morning. I might see you, then . . .'

Vivien had forgotten everything else, and it wasn't until she was waving goodbye to her escort as he executed a dashing turn in the street that she realised the time. Nine o'clock—and it hadn't even occurred to her to ring through and explain why she would be late! She raised her hand to the doorbell with a smile curving her lips at the unlikely, but true, explanation she would have to give. The rest of the day had gone into a blur and it seemed almost strange that she was still carrying a bag of damp bathing things, which she would have forgotten entirely if someone hadn't thoughtfully thrust them at her out of the bus.

The door opened abruptly and Justin, looking icy, stood back to let her come in. He was speaking before she had time to open her mouth.

'No doubt you'd forgotten you were supposed to be on duty at six?' There was a bite in the words. 'Or, probably, that you'd come here to work at all? My sister may run her staff on a very light rein, but when she had particularly indicated that she wants you here at a certain time, don't you think you might at least have the courtesy to obey?'

'I—I'm sorry. I hadn't realized how late it was getting——'

'No doubt you found other attractions to make it seem unimportant. But may I remind you that you're actually being paid to work certain hours?'

The sting in his tone brought Vivien's chin up. All at once there was no way she was going to give any explanations to him. Let him jump to whatever conclusions he liked! 'I'll go and make my excuses to Mona,' she said stiffly, with the remembered pain in her heart making her give him back glare for glare.

'Mona's out, or had you forgotten that too? *I* put PJ to bed—and there's no need for you to go up and see him. I rather think you've worn out your usefulness here. In fact I suggest we consider your contract terminated as of now—on the grounds of bad timekeeping and irresponsibility!'

Vivien whirled back to face him. 'My contract's with your sister,' she brought out in a sudden blaze, 'not with you, so you have no right to sack me! Mrs Mantagna can, if she cares to! In fact I resign, it's time I went home anyway! Philip doesn't need nursing any more, and I agree with you, my presence *has* stopped being useful. I shall ask Mrs Mantagna to arrange a flight home for me as soon as possible.'

'Good. Or do you plan to ask her for an open-ended ticket, so that you can stay on and simply enjoy yourself while making as much out of her as possible?'

Vivien stepped forward with every intention of slapping his face out of her red rage, but the peal of the telephone stopped her. As Justin moved to answer it she turned on her heel and ran up the stairs, with tears of fury and hurt stinging her eyes. She heard him say,

'Mamma? Oh, hallo—no, I'm not out of breath, it must be the line. You're ringing from Boston, are you? How's everything over there? I see, you're ringing to say you're coming back—"

The slam of Vivien's bedroom door shut off his voice. She raged across the room. She couldn't care less if he was talking to his mother and his whole family was welcome to him. All she wanted to do was go home.

She would, too, as soon as Mona could arrange a flight for her. She wouldn't go with the sack, though, and if Justin so much as suggested it she'd claim unfair dismissal. She wished she'd never come here at all . . . except for delivering that baby this afternoon, which was still a triumphant memory and touched with magic.

She wasn't asleep when she heard Mona's footsteps come along the corridor and hesitate outside her room. She didn't tap as Vivien's light was off. Vivien could imagine that she had come in and been faced with Justin demanding Vivien's instant dismissal. She wondered how Mona had taken that—and then didn't care, about any of them. She *would* go home, and she had done quite enough for Mona and Zack for them to do without her from now on!

Since she hadn't accepted the sack, Vivien got up with determination in the morning to go and have breakfast with Philip in his room as usual. 'I'm sorry I wasn't here last night, but I was in a bus accident. And you're the first person I've told,' she added, trying to keep grimness out of her voice, and knowing how much it would please him to hear the news before anyone else.

'Was anyone killed?' he asked with a ghoulish hopefulness.

'No, no one was even bleeding! You really are a little horror, aren't you?' She managed a grin at him. 'We just skidded badly, that's all. Nearly turned over, and everyone was thrown about a lot, but—' She turned her head as the door opened. 'Oh, good morning, Dr Laurens. You're early!'

Justin came into the room on the Maltese doctor's heels, looking smooth and blank. Vivien immediately stiffened into rigidity, but Philip was too full of news to notice.

'Dr Laurens, Vivien was in a bus accident yesterday! You ought to examine her instead of me!'

'I gather you weren't hurt, Nurse Vivien?' Dr Laurens gave her a wide smile. 'Though if you have any bruises I'll be glad to treat the heroine of the hour!' He turned to Philip without seeing the way Justin's head had turned sharply in Vivien's direction. 'Yes, I've heard about the accident, Philip, it was up at Xemxija. And this young lady who looks after you so well delivered a tiny baby too, for one of my other patients, as it happens. Did she tell you about that?'

'I was just going to,' Vivien said hastily as she saw Philip's face cloud accusingly. 'It—it was the climax of the story and we hadn't got to it yet.'

'Well, I'm afraid news travels fast, Philip, so you can't be first for once! I've had a whole family telling me how wonderful your nurse is. And,' Dr Laurens went on, glancing round with a smile which included both Vivien and Justin, 'there's now a baby girl who's going to be christened Josefina Conspicua Viviane, so your name will continue on our island, Nurse Vivien, even if it will be adapted to our spelling!'

'Really? Oh, I never thought they'd do that! The baby is all right, isn't she? The hospital seemed to think —Well, while I was there they said she was fine, but I was going to ask if I could ring up later and check.'

'Josefina Conspicua Viviane is doing very well, thank you, and so is her mother. Her father is still somewhat in a state of shock and lighting candles in every church —several to give thanks for you, and at least one for the bus driver, I should imagine!' Dr Laurens said comfortably. 'Apparently it's a miracle he managed not to turn the bus over. The other driver was very thoroughly to blame, I hear. Some of these young tearabouts, eh, Justin?'

'Yes, they can be dangerous. I hadn't heard about the accident—Vivien seems to keep her own counsel. Except to PJ. No doubt she knew how much he'd like to be ahead of the rest of us.' Justin's voice had a jerk in it, but as Vivien carefully wasn't looking at him she couldn't see his expression. 'What time did all this happen?'

'The crash was at about half past four, I believe—yes? With no real casualties, I'm glad to say, except for bumps and bruises and a few sprains. But Nurse Vivien should be allowed some extra rest today after the shock, I suggest. You must have kept your nerve very well, my dear, for I remember your telling me that midwifery wasn't part of your particular training.' Dr Laurens gave Vivien another approving look and turned, at last, to Philip. 'Let's have a look at the patient I came to see, though I must say he seems so well recovered that I'm not sure I shall need to pay him any more visits!'

Vivien managed to leave the room while Justin and Dr Laurens were still in it, on the excuse of removing something which had got left behind from the breakfast tray. All the same she was caught by Dr Laurens when he came downstairs again with Justin beside him. The Maltese doctor paused to offer kindly to examine Vivien in case she was suffering from any bad bruises. She assured him she wasn't and then had to wait while he asked her to convey his apologies to Mona for calling so early before she was up. Then he was leaving, and Vivien was halfway up the stairs before Justin's rapid footsteps caught up with her.

'Vivien——'

'Yes, Dr Baron? Unless you want me for something special,' Vivien said with icy rapidity, 'I'm on duty. My resignation doesn't take effect yet since I haven't seen your sister yet.'

'I apologise for what I said,' he began stiffly. 'I was——'

'It really doesn't make any difference. I still want to

leave. It's time I did!' Vivien retorted, and swept rapidly away from him to go back to Philip. It was only after she had got there that she remembered it wasn't logical for her to want to leave if she was supposed to be so keen on Zack—but that had somehow stopped mattering, and she certainly wasn't going to take anything back.

She had been afraid Philip would now want to know all sorts of obstetrical details, but luckily his interest had been overtaken by another piece of news. Uncle Justin had told him his grandmother was coming back at the end of this week. He was full of all the things he was going to tell her, and various flights of fancy about what present she might bring him from America. Vivien wondered drily whether she and Justin's mother would pass on the tarmac. If Lady Baron was as fierce as Mona's mother-in-law she wasn't sure if she wanted to meet her, Philip's obvious devotion to her notwithstanding.

She managed to catch Mona mid-morning, carefully leaving Philip amusing himself out of earshot with his car-racing track, which they had just laid all around the dining-room. There was no sign of Justin, but Mona must have talked to him, because she had heard about the accident.

'You could have been dreadfully hurt!' she said distractedly, but looking rather as if she wasn't listening to anything Vivien said. 'Thank Goodness you weren't! Jus said the bus nearly went over or something, and then there was a baby you saved—poor little thing, I hope it wasn't hurt. Vivien, don't worry about working today, I'm sure we can manage——'

'What I was trying to say was that I'd like to go home,' Vivien repeated patiently. 'It's nothing to do with the accident, only that—that it's time I did. And as for . . . for the other matter, I'm sure you've got far enough——'

'Oh yes, and besides, Zack says—Well, never mind

that now. You'll—you'll just stay a few more days, won't you? I mean, until we can fix a flight? And don't say anything to Pip about going, will you, it might upset him.'

'I shouldn't think it will, he's got far too much of a crush on Zack to miss me. And he's excited about his grandmother coming home. Still, I won't tell him, of course. I'd just like to have a flight out as soon as possible, that's all.'

'Yes, all right. Justin will fix it. Oh, there's the phone! Excuse me, Vivien—and *do* rest, as much as you need, you must be awfully shaken!'

It wasn't exactly a satisfactory interview, and it was foolish to feel put down because Mona seemed to take the thought of her departure almost casually. She seemed to be in an exceptionally fluttery mood this morning. Justin in a rage and the thought of her mother's return no doubt explained that, but all the same she might have shown *some* regret.

The next two days dragged unbearably. Zack didn't put in an appearance, which sent Philip into a state of disappointment. Mona was distrait and had stopped confiding anything. Justin had taken to regarding Vivien grimly, but that might have been due to her habit of sweeping past him whenever they met, and never addressing him directly, as much as anything. Presumably he *was* seeing to her flight home. On the third day Mona said suddenly that she was going to take Philip out with her and would be gone 'at least until late afternoon' so Vivien could be free. Vivien stayed in her room all the rest of the morning, and then for the early part of the afternoon, torn between a desire to pack and a knowledge that it would be pointless until she was actually going. Then it occurred to her that she might actually seem to be hiding, which was enough to fetch her out for a walk round Valletta.

She wandered through the streets with a feeling of

farewell, consciously drawing in the city's beauty to remember and trying not to feel she would be wiser to forget the whole place. Memory stabbed: Justin saying to her on her first day, 'You look like someone who's prepared to fall in love with the whole island . . .' If only she had stuck to that, instead of losing her heart foolishly to more than Malta.

She drew her breath on a sharp sigh and tried to think staunchly that she would be glad to be busy again. There must be a hospital somewhere where she could go and work and become so totally absorbed that nothing else mattered.

She found her feet had taken her to the wall that overlooked Grand Harbour. She hesitated, shrugged wryly and then mounted to the view which had marked her first day. From here she had seen her first *dghasa*—and Justin had pulled the pins out of her hair and kissed her . . .

'I wandered lonely as a cloud?' a voice said. 'And why alone, I wonder?'

Justin was there, a yard away, dark hair ruffled by the sea wind and green eyes narrowed to watch her. Vivien's mouth went suddenly dry. She managed to snap back into herself and move sharply away from the rail.

'I didn't see you—' she began.

'No, obviously not. I was just along there. I like this view—do you?'

'It's attractive, I suppose. I hadn't meant to walk this far. Excuse me for disturbing you, I must get back now.'

'You're very unforgiving, aren't you? And you won't acknowledge that anyone else might have a temper as unreasonable as your own!'

'I hadn't even thought about it. Anyway, one gets used to doctors having unreasonable tempers—when one's a paid employee.' There was an ache that seemed to settle like a leaden weight in Vivien's stomach. 'Do you happen to know whether your sister's arranged anything about my flight home?'

'She's left it to me. As it's the height of the tourist season now things aren't as easy as all that. However, I'll walk back with you now and do some more telephoning about it—since your departure is a matter of interest to us both!'

That stung too much to allow an answer, and they walked back in silence with Vivien refusing to allow herself to look at him, and speeding her steps to briskness. It was a relief when they reached the house and Justin's key in the lock let them both into the wide marble-floored hall. Then, before Vivien could retreat to her room, Anna came out through the double doors from the drawing-room in a rush with a flush staining the olive skin of her cheeks.

The maid stopped on seeing Justin. She broke abruptly into indignant speech.

'Please, sir, is it right that Mr Mantagna accuses me of lying? I say Madami is not in her room, and she *isn't*! how can he tell me to "go up and look again"? Madami has not been in since this morning, I told him so!'

'All right, Anna, I'll deal with it. Go back to the kitchen, and don't worry. And you have my apologies, on Mr Mantagna's behalf!'

For some reason Justin seemed to want Vivien to go ahead of him into the drawing-room, since his arm stopped her from turning away to go upstairs. Charles Mantagna was standing in front of the fireplace looking plumply angry, and the sight of Vivien didn't seem to improve his temper. Justin, however, spoke before he could.

'Charles, do I gather you've taken to being rude to my sister's staff?' he enquired in a dangerously smooth tone.

'Mona seems quite incapable of disciplining her servants,' Charles Mantagna retorted, a venomous glance at Vivien showing he definitely included her in that category. 'And I do not wish, Justin, to be flatly told by *my inferiors* that your sister is not in! How can that be true, when she knew I would be calling round this afternoon?'

'If Mona's out she's out. Did she actually grant you this appointment, or did you merely instruct her that you were coming?'

Charles Mantagna's mouth opened and shut again at Justin's dry tone. It was plain that he had expected to find an ally in another male and was both disconcerted and angry that it shouldn't be so. He rallied and began stiffly,

'Your sister knows I always call at a certain time. This is understood between us. Furthermore, I am certain that she is actually in the house, because it would be most unlike her to go out all day when I am expecting to see her.'

'I'm not sure if she said when she'd be back, so all I can suggest is that you make your appointments more carefully in future. All *I* know is that she's gone out and taken Philip with her—do you know any more than that, Vivien?'

Vivien was certain he was only asking because doing so would be guaranteed to annoy Charles Mantagna. She had no objection to joining in that, even if it was Justin who had started it. 'Late afternoon, I think, was when she said she might come back,' she said, wrinkling her brow and looking helpful. 'Though of course she might not. She does have quite a lot of friends she might go and see, and although it's nearly five now you'd better not wait!'

Nothing could be more certain than that Charles would loathe being told not to wait by a mere employee. He was beginning to puff himself up—but there was the sound of the front door opening, on Mona's voice, and Philip's. And Zack's.

Vivien felt as if she ought to deliver some kind of warning, but she was too late. An extremely cheerful trio appeared in the doorway. Mona's face was radiant, Philip's was sparkling—and Zack had his arm round Mona's shoulders.

They paused. Charles Mantagna recovered from his shock. 'Mona,' he said quickly, and very very coldly, 'I believe I should have a word with you alone. Or with your brother present, perhaps!'

'No, you won't speak to her alone,' Zack said calmly. 'Mantagna, isn't it? Mona's trustee?' His arm stayed round Mona and his other hand hushed Philip, who subsided at once and put on an expression somewhere between smug and lofty. Vivien could see that they had told him . . . but Zack was going on. 'If you want to talk to Mona in future you can do it in front of me.'

'Then let me say here and and now that as trustee, I have the power to see that not one cent of my cousin's money can be touched by any fortune-hunter!'

The vicious note in Charles Mantagna's voice brought nothing but a placid smile from Zack. 'I should think so,' he said approvingly. 'It ought to go into a trust for young Phil, if anything. And since I've got more cash than I know what to do with, I'm hardly likely to want to touch hers, now am I? As far as I'm concerned I couldn't care less if she hadn't got a penny! In fact, seeing the trouble it causes, I'd sooner she hadn't!'

'I hardly think anyone would believe——'

'No, you don't think much, do you?' Zack's long dark curls gave a rueful shake; the silver earring glinted. 'But I'd take yourself off if I were you and stop trying to bully people. What does it take—a pay-off? Mona, love, do you want to get some papers drawn up to give this character free rein with your late husband's cash? It's entirely up to you, but I reckon that's what he's after!'

That was too much for Charles Mantagna. His face turned apoplectic and for a moment Vivien thought he might have a stroke. He managed, 'Mona, I shall telephone your mother——'

'Oh, you needn't bother to do that, she's on her way back,' Justin's voice broke in blandly, speaking for the first time. He glanced across at his sister. 'Hence the haste? The announcement *now*? You really are an idiot child, why didn't you tell me what was going on?'

'Oh, Jus, I thought you'd only say——'

'Then you don't know me very well after all these years!' Justin told her trenchantly. He looked at Zack thoughtfully. 'Of course I hardly know you yet, and we seem to have met on a false premise up to now, but if you're my sister's choice I'll back you. Particularly since you look calm enough to cope with her!'

Zack gave his attractive grin. 'Thanks, but no need, if you don't want to put yourself out. We got married at noon today. It's all licensed and legal. Catholic too—my brother's a priest and he's over on a visit, so he took the ceremony.'

There was a choking sound from Charles Mantagna. Justin glanced briefly over her shoulder to say, 'Oh, go away, Charles!' He drew Mona and Zack and Philip out of the doorway to clear the path as Charles Mantagna drew himself up to his full height and stalked out. No one even bothered to watch him go, and Justin went on talking. 'I'll say congratulations, then. How many people were in on this secret?'

'Vivien—' Mona was suddenly drawing her into the circle, with a guilty look that didn't manage to dim the radiance in her eyes. She went on very rapidly, 'She didn't want to lie, but I begged her to because it seemed to be the only way out. You're not to blame her, Jus, I'm sure she would have told you if I hadn't particularly asked her not to, and——'

'I'll say congratulations too and leave you all to talk about it,' Vivien brought out at speed. She added, 'And nobody had to persuade me, I was perfectly happy about it! Excuse me now, I'm sure you want to have a family conference. Mona, Zack, I'm delighted you've actually gone and done it—and Philip, I bet you're delighted too!'

She wanted to get out of there fast, because Justin had turned to look at her with a gleam in his eye, and Mona was making far too much of a meal of things. Vivien managed a grin at Philip as she passed him, but then she was pulling the drawing-room door shut behind her and making for the stairs. She heard the door immediately open again and then Justin's voice.

'Not so fast! Come back down here!'

'I'm sure you want to talk to your sister——'

'No, I don't, I want to talk to you!' He had reached her, and caught her wrist in a steely grip. 'And as there's never any peace in this house we'll go out—now!'

He pulled her back down the stairs, called out, 'Mona, I'm borrowing the car again, so you'd better not want it!' and didn't wait for an answer. He already had the door open which led through to the garage opening through a high arched doorway on to the street, and a moment later had pushed Vivien hard towards the passenger door of the car.

'Get in—it's open. Get in, I said!'

Her heart was sending up a fast uneven thud as she did as he said. He probably only wanted to tell her off . . . He backed rapidly out into the street and gunned the engine into a road, then they were off, threading through the streets at a speed which made her bite her lip.

Within moments they were swooping out through the high arch in Valletta's landward wall. A swing round the massive fountain that graced the square, a swoop past the Phoenicia Hotel, and Justin was putting his foot down still further to hurtle down the smooth sweep of road which edged Ta' Xbiex yacht basin.

'Where—where are we going?' asked Vivien.

'Who knows? I just happen to be on this road. And don't talk to me while I'm driving!'

That was cool, considering she hadn't even chosen to be here. Suddenly she didn't care. The sunroof of the car was open and the wind tangled her hair against her cheeks. A wild beat in her blood told her she would go with him anywhere, and she was tired of fighting against it. He took a sharp turn that almost flung her against him and then they were leaving streets behind and travelling inland, with rocky countryside whipping by as they climbed. Then the road was dropping again, turning almost into a track, and the sea was spread bluely out ahead of them with a shimmer as it merged mistily into the horizon.

Justin pulled abruptly off the road on to dusty yellow earth with a tuft of dry grass here and there. He killed the engine, then stared at the emptiness around them with satisfaction.

'A suitably quiet spot. I've even given us a view. Now, Vivien—' His head turned, and green eyes with a glint in them regarded her. 'Now, and uninterrupted, we talk!'

'What—what about?'

'You and me. And don't say there's no such thing as you and me, because you know damn well there is! No, on second thoughts, let's start with the only way I ever do get any sense out of you!'

His arms reached for her and the spinning delight was back, the urgent excitement running like a thread between them, the fierce pleasure of his lips on hers and a joy to melt her bones. Vivien's fingers tangled into the hair behind his ears and she could feel the race of his heartbeat against her own. She kissed him back without caring what she was showing and when he drew away, a little but not far enough to let her out of his arms, his voice when he spoke was husky and breathless.

'Then why, for pity's sake, do I have to fly in from Saudi Arabia and pick up a local newspaper at the airport, only to find that you're apparently "pop star Zack

Delaney's new girlfriend"? Don't tell me it was only because my sister begged you not to tell me—you were throwing up barriers against me again, weren't you? And just when I was beginning to think I'd managed to get you to treat me like a human being!'

'Well . . .'

He felt her slight withdrawal and though his arms prevented it a rueful look crept in to join the exasperation in his eyes. 'We're back to Caroline again, are we? Oh dear——'

'I just wasn't minded to act as an entertainment,' said Vivien. 'A substitute.'

'You're not a substitute. You never were. *She* was.' The words were prompt, though the ruefulness increased in his eyes. 'I can't say I meant to interfere with love's young dream, though I must say no one would have thought . . . Without wishing to sound conceited, my love—' the word sent a tremor along Vivien's nerves —'your friend really does believe in chasing! I'm only human, and when a pretty girl makes it as clear as day that she wants my company, including telephoning me at frequent intervals—and when *you* wouldn't give me so much as the time of day——'

'You didn't particularly want me to!'

'Didn't I? It was you I fancied right from the start. I've always had a weakness for dark girls,' Justin added mischievously, and his lips brushed hers briefly as if to still her protest. 'Only then I lost you your job by an injudicious remark, and you were flaming mad. It was *you* I rang up, after giving you time to calm down. I got Caroline, which was disconcerting in the extreme. Curiosity—and politeness—turned that into a date, and then lo and behold there you were, glaring at me again. I employed you to look after Philip at the Harraday, which seemed a good way of getting to know you, but——'

'But you went on taking Caroline out, and don't tell

me you were all that unwilling. Did she really keep ringing you up?'

'Yes. I suspect you don't know your friend as well as you think you do. Oh yes, I did play along—but then you'd barely speak to me, would you, except when you were actually nursing! You did forget to freeze me sometimes then. But, of course, there was your doorstep scene with whatsisname——'

'Tom,' Vivien said helpfully.

'Yes. The one who's threatening to knock my block off. If he wasn't a good four inches taller than I am, I might have felt the same about him. Except,' Justin added smoothly, 'that saying you're "fond of" someone is a dead giveaway!'

'I am fond of him. And of Caroline. I hope they'll be very happy together.'

'So do I. I also wish him luck,' said Justin drily, and went on quickly as he felt Vivien stir. 'I decided the only thing to do was to sweep you out here to get you away from Caroline *and* whatsisname. However, on the plane you started treating me like a two-headed monster all over again—which always makes me behave like one . . . People do, you know.' He drew his head back to look down deeply into her eyes, with a warmth in his own that made Vivien feel dizzy. 'You've been making my life thoroughly difficult,' he said softly, 'and once or twice I've quite decided to give up. And then found I couldn't. You with your long witch hair and your blue eyes deep enough to drown in . . . Is it surprising I was about to try the same trick in reverse, and sweep you away from here to get you away from this latest man you appeared to have collected when I only took my eyes off you for six days?'

'You—you were what? I thought I was just going back to England——'

'With me, and not necessarily to England. I'm sure I could find some excuse why we had to go via somewhere else. Anywhere else which wasn't full of your friends and my family! Somewhere where I could keep you still long enough to propose to you—if you'd listen! And yes, I do mean it—all the conventional bit, moonlight and roses, till death us do part, the lot. Why, my darling girl, would you never let it occur to you that I might be serious?'

'Because I always thought you were out of my league. I mean . . .' The look of extreme bewilderment he was giving her was bringing a bubble of happiness close to bursting point inside her. 'Well, you do look—I mean . . .'

'Will you stop saying "I mean" and talk some sense? Oh, good God, you haven't gone and caught Mona's nonsense through being out here?' The look of total exasperation in Justin's eyes brought Vivien to the edge of laughter. 'And besides, if it's money you're talking about, it's my sister who's obnoxiously rich, not me. I'll admit I've earned a bomb lately—and hope to go on doing so—but I work for what I get! Let alone that it's all quite irrelevant, that doesn't put me out of anyone's league, let alone yours! I love you, and you must have grasped that—this afternoon if no other time!'

'I love you too,' Vivien assured him. 'It was just that——'

'Thank goodness, an admission!' He drew her close again, his lips hovering over hers. 'No one would have thought so, darling, the way you went for me after my fit of jealousy the other night, and the way you've treated me since. You wouldn't even accept my apology, would you? And you might have thought that I'd been going out of my mind with worry!'

'Were you?' Vivien asked with surprise.

'Of course I was! I'd been imagining you lying injured in a ditch at least, after coming off the back of that damned man's motorbike. Then you came in looking shiny-eyed as if you'd merely been spending your time being kissed—Let's forget about all that. This is now, and you haven't yet said whether you'll marry me!'

'You haven't actually asked me . . .'

'Will you?'

'Yes,' she said promptly, and looked up at him with all her love in her eyes. She saw his darken and then his lips reached hers again, sealing the happiness that spread through her in a thunder of joy and need, longing and promised fulfilment.